The Chess Piece Magician

The Chess Piece Magician

Douglas Bruton

Kelpies

Kelpies is an imprint of Floris Books

This edition published in 2009 by Floris Books
© 2009 Douglas Bruton

Douglas Bruton has asserted his right under
the Copyright, Designs and Patents Act 1988
to be identified as the Author of this Work.

The publisher acknowledges a Lottery grant
from the Scottish Arts Council towards the
publication of this series.

British Library CIP Data available

ISBN 978-086315-701-1

Printed in Poland

For Ben, Daniel and Sam, who had this story first
— because it was for them.

Contents

1. The Found Thing

They always came to Uig. On the same slow boat across to the island. Along the same winding roads from the east of Lewis to the west. All the way to nowhere. All the way to Uig and a village there. Every year they came for the same two weeks of the summer and stayed in the same cottage; the same cottage with its small grey windows squinting out over the same bright blue Atlantic that broke in a ragged foaming line on the same white, sandy beach.

"There she is!" said Corrie's father as always when the car crested the hill and they made-believe that they could see all the way to America. Corrie never understood if by "she" his father meant the ocean or the cottage.

The cottage was the last in a strung out, crooked line of cottages all facing the sea. Their windows like staring eyes, never blinking.

"Taste that air, Corrie!" said his father, winding down the driver's window and leaning his head half out of the car. "If you could bottle that and sell it, you'd soon be a rich man!"

Corrie couldn't taste anything, not unless "cold" counted as a flavour. He pulled the sleeves of his sweater down over his knuckles and shuffled deeper into the corner of his seat, as far away from the open window as he could squeeze.

Corrie's father brought the car to an abrupt halt half way down the hill that led to the cottages and leaped out.

"I'll walk from here, I think," he said, bobbing his head back in at the open door. "If that's okay?"

Corrie's mother nodded, waving him away as she inched awkwardly from the passenger seat into the driver seat. She looked at Corrie in the rear-view mirror and smiled. "Every year …," she said, pulling the door shut and grinding the car into first gear.

"Why *every* year?" said Corrie, cupping his hands together and blowing into them with exaggeration.

Corrie's mother wound up the window, jerking the car into second gear with the same grating of metal that had sounded when she had put it into first.

"He likes to come upon Uig *slowly,*" she replied. "He likes to savour the timeless quality of the place … register the changes … take it all in … and announce his return. The place demands it."

His dad's words spilled out of his mum's mouth, making it sound like some grand triumphal march into a thronging city. Aside from the row of cottages, this part of Uig boasted a post office, that resembled one of the corrugated sheds bordering his dad's allotment at home, and a small corner shop converted from a household garage.

"No," said Corrie, "I mean ... why do we come here every year?"

"Not *every* year, Corr," said his mother, side-stepping the question.

It had not been *every* year. They hadn't come the year Corrie had caught chicken pox. It was the best summer Corrie could remember. They had got out all the photographs of Uig and pinned them up around the house to cheer up his dad. In photographs, the turquoise blue of the sea, trapped and still, without the biting wind, looked inviting and exotic, needing only a feathery palm tree to complete the illusion. The sun-kissed sandy beach trailing away to infinity, empty and oh-so-white, seemed like some vision of holiday paradise. Even the sky was blue ... at least in the photographs they had taken. Corrie's father and mother had waxed lyrical over the holiday they had missed that year, but despite the constant itching of his crusty rash and the enforced isolation of quarantine — not unlike the time spent in Uig — Corrie had smiled and thanked the Chicken Pox God for preventing the annual summer pilgrimage.

The fact is that Corrie was not fooled by the cunning deception worked by his dad's camera. A photograph could not capture the slow, dull passage of the long days in Uig, where there was nothing to do and no one to do it with. The wind-tossed sea and the wind-torn beach did not encourage the usual family posturing that Corrie saw in his friends' summer snaps where children danced almost naked around extravagant sandcastles. Apart from one year, when the sun had scorched the heather and the sand had burnt the soles of Corrie's feet, in all their family pictures of Uig they were smothered under heavy coats and hats. Worst of all, there wasn't even a television in the cottage.

"It's good to get away from it all!" his father said over and over again.

Corrie did not agree.

The car swung off the road and crunched over the gravel drive.

"Here we are!" said his mother, wrenching the handbrake so that the car lurched to a sudden stop.

"I expect you'll want to get off to the beach, Corrie. I'll open up the house and you can fetch us some firewood, eh?" she said, swinging round in her seat to face him.

Corrie smiled weakly, got quietly out of the car, nudged the door shut again with his hip and headed towards the sea.

"Your coat, Corrie ... don't forget your coat!" called his mother, now rummaging amongst the blankets and the boxes of food that filled the boot.

"There you go!" she said, holding his coat up in the air. "See you in a little while then," and she disappeared back into the confusion of spaghetti packs and pillowcases.

Corrie's hair was sticking up at the back, pressed into uneven brown spikes where he had slept in the back seat of the car. He was not yet tall and his legs and arms were thin. "Thin as sticks," his dad sometimes joked. Zipping his coat up to his chin, he retraced his steps to the bottom of the drive. Looking right, he could see his father just coming level with the first cottage. He waved, but Corrie pretended he hadn't seen and crossed the track that called itself a road, making for the beach.

It was always his job to collect wood for the fire, the only task he regularly, if also reluctantly, undertook. Sometimes he had to walk a great way along the sand before he found enough driftwood to fuel the open fireplace. Sometimes, after the sea had thrashed itself quiet against the beach, after Corrie had been woken by the wind shaking the loose pane of glass in the bedroom window, allowing the cold breath of outside into the room, then there was no need to walk more than a few paces in either direction to collect an armful of good firewood. On those occasions, all kinds of flotsam and jetsam littered the sand as far as you could see. Of most use were the split and broken packing cases from passing ships, that had once carried oranges or bananas, or the heavy wooden forklift pallets and the thick remains of shipping crates with foreign names burnt into the wood like cattle brands.

After the storm times, there was treasure to be found: crusty pink-mouthed shells churned up from far out to sea and flung carelessly onto the sand; mermaid's purses that popped when you squeezed them; polished fragments of mother of pearl with little rainbows dancing over the shiny surface; old lace-less boots that had their own stories to tell;

and strange bottles with their labels washed off. One year, he had found a roughly carved, wooden head with a yawning crack running through the middle of one eye and down its left cheek. His dad had said it was probably part of a figurehead from an old boat. "We should look it up somewhere," he had suggested to Corrie, but they never did. The head had been placed on the mantelpiece in the cottage where the crack in its face deepened and its bright paint blistered and flaked.

But today, the beach was bare save for the white, bark-stripped, twisted serpent sticks that would do nothing more than crackle and spit on the fire before dissolving to thin ash in a moment so short that the heat from their burning would be barely felt. Corrie turned to the left, walking along the sand away from the cottages. To his right, the sea hissed and sighed, rushing up to Corrie's shoes before slipping away again. The road was hidden behind a bank of dunes held together with spiky tufts of marram grass and, behind them, a long way off, a jagged line of peaks lifted themselves up into the air. A bird cried a mournful cry then tumbled out of view.

"Lapwing," said Corrie with authority, without breaking step. Two summers ago, they had found a book in the cottage listing all the birds that nested on the island, and Corrie and his dad had become instant ornithologists. They had borrowed binoculars from the rust-haired old lady who tended the sheep that wandered over the purple hills. She lived in the first of the straggling line of cottages with an over excited black and white dog that nipped your heels as you passed, as though you were a stray sheep.

"You go careful now," the red-haired lady had cautioned them.

They had spent a week crouched in ditches or sneaking up hills in the early hours of the morning when everyone else slept, sustained by limp sandwiches wrapped in paper parcels and flasks of hot sweet tea, their ears pricked to catch the briefest snatch of song, their eyes straining for the merest glimpse of feather. They had ticked each bird off one by one on a strip of paper that unravelled like a long supermarket till receipt and Corrie had taken some unsuccessful pictures with his dad's camera.

He had been persuaded to ask for his own binoculars the following Christmas, but for most of the year they hung in a heavy brown leather case on the back of his bedroom door. He had brought them with him again this time ... but only because his dad had packed them.

Corrie gathered together small bundles of the sticks, leaving them piled in little mounds at intervals high up on the beach. He would collect them on his way back if he had not found anything more substantial.

He stooped to pick something shiny out of the sand ... a shell. He ran his fingers over the smooth polished inside of the shell. It was cold and felt like glass. He held it to one ear and pressed his other ear closed with one finger, listening for the *shush shush* of the sea-memory trapped inside. It always made him smile ... more than the real sea did, splashing again and again at his feet. He put it into his jacket pocket — his first piece of summer treasure — then continued his search for firewood.

Further along the beach he spotted, wedged half in and half out of the sand, a long thick piece of wood, square like a fence post and bent over.

Just the thing! thought Corrie running up the beach with his legs lifting high like a hurdler. The post was lying well clear of the waterline and almost at the foot of the first dunes. Corrie began tugging at it, twisting it first one way and then the other, shaking it back and forth. He wrapped his arms around the post and pulled hard, his legs splayed wide and his feet sliding in the sand. But his grip was not tight enough and it gave only a little. Corrie kicked at it with the underside of his shoe, then climbed onto the outstretched finger of wood, bouncing up and down on the end until suddenly it split in two with a sharp tearing crack that sent Corrie sprawling onto his hands and knees. He rolled over to look at the splintered stubby point now sticking out of the sand, hearing his dad's voice gently admonishing his bull-headed efforts, "Brains not brawn, Corrie!"

He crawled over to beside the still-buried end of the post and began digging away the sand from around it with his hands. "Be easier to carry in two bits anyway," he muttered to himself as if justifying the brawn. The post was longer than he had thought and, if he managed to dig it clear, might be sufficient to feed the fire that night, without the other piles of sticks. He brushed the loose sand further back from his excavations using the flat sweep of his forearm. Although some way from the high tide mark, the sand underneath was damp and so did not fall back in on itself. He scraped at it with his hands. The hole quickly deepened around the post and Corrie stopped every now and again to push at the stubborn root. It moved a little more each time.

At last he stood up and took another grip at it, certain that now he could pull it clear. Heaving it, inch by slow inch, out of the clinging sand, finally it jerked free.

The hole it had left in the ground winked up at Corrie like the blinking black eye of a giant beast. He lifted the wooden post clear and knelt over the gap. Corrie breathed in the smell, trying to locate the memory of it. The space was filling with a black-brown oily fluid. He leaned closer seeing his own shadow distorted in the deep dark liquid pupil, an ill-defined halo of reflected sky curling and uncurling about his head. Something else caught Corrie's attention, but this time it was not a shiny white shell. He flattened his body against the opening and reached one arm as far into the hole as he could. His fingers closed on something hard sticking out from one side of the hole. He tugged at it and it came away so easily that Corrie almost dropped it into the black brackish pool at the bottom.

The object was like an overlarge ice-hockey puck, a little battered and imperfect perhaps, and larger than the palm of Corrie's hand. He rubbed it in the dry sand to wipe it clean of the dark mud that clung to it. He lifted it up again, running his palm over one surface. There was something there. It was difficult to see, so slight was the marking, but his fingers felt the lightest impression of an embossed image; a raised pattern of lines, that coiled in and out of one another like a braided circle of rope, or a twisted ring of snakes. He turned it over. The other side was much rougher with no such marking.

"Dè tha agad an sin?" came a voice from above.

He looked up to see a girl staring down at him, her red hair across her face like a veil. She tried tucking it back behind one ear but it blew free again. She was maybe as tall as Corrie, though standing at the top of the dune with her feet planted squarely in the sand she looked both taller and a little older.

"Dè tha agad an sin?" she said again.

It was like music, Corrie thought. *All sound and no meaning.*

"What?" he said.

"Oh, you're a visitor too!" she said, and though she spoke now in English her voice still carried the sing-song rise and fall of the Gaelic.

Corrie did not reply.

"What have you found then … some treasure?" she asked, sitting down on the top of the dune.

"Treasure?" said Corrie, "What treasure?"

"I'm Kat."

"Kat," parroted Corrie.

"Yes … with a 'k,'" she added.

"Kat with a 'k?'" Corrie did not understand the significance.

"Kat … short for Katrine," she explained, rolling

her eyes, turning the corners of her mouth down to signal her disapproval.

"Oh," said Corrie.

"On holiday ... sort of. Came yesterday ... for two weeks," she continued in a sort of clipped shorthand.

"You said something about treasure," said Corrie.

"I was meaning the thing in your hand. Thought maybe you'd found some Viking hoard. It's been known hereabouts."

Corrie tried to slip the found object into his jacket pocket without drawing attention to it.

"I'm collecting wood for the fire," he said, changing the subject. "I just dug up this post ... see?"

Kat slid down the sandy slope. The hole was now half full of the brown-black liquid and the dark sides of the hole were crumbling in on themselves.

"Stinks a bit," she said.

"Yes, it does rather." Corrie was happy to divert the conversation away from the object in his pocket.

"Like rotten vegetables!"

"Yeah," he replied, though he knew that this was not really an accurate description of the smell. It was a smell he recognised, but could not quite locate.

An awkward silence followed. The children stared down into the black hole. Even the sea seemed to hold its breath. Waiting. *Waiting,* he thought, *for him to reveal the treasure he had found.* Corrie did not know what it was he had in his pocket but he knew he wanted it to himself.

"I found a shell," he said, at last breaking the quiet.

"Is this the wood then?" Kat asked, ignoring his announcement and lifting the broken short end of the post.

Corrie nodded. "I'd best be getting back with it." He got to his feet.

"I'll give you a hand if you like," she said.

Corrie shrugged, picked up one end of the larger length of wood and, dragging it behind him, he set off back along the beach with Kat keeping step beside him. They walked a while without speaking, Corrie with his head bowed, his eyes focused on the sand just in front, and Kat looking out over the sea, all the while stealing glances at Corrie. Overhead the clouds were thickening, glowering grey and dark. The blue of the sea had deepened into a dirty grey-blue, and the waves smacked again and again on the dulled beach.

Kat stopped and pointed out across the sea.

"*Seall!*" she said.

"What?" Corrie didn't understand.

"Look!" she insisted.

Corrie looked to where she pointed, but saw nothing. He glanced at the far horizon. He could no longer tell where the sea ended and the sky began.

"*Sèididh a' gaoth gu cruaidh a-nochd.*"

"What?" said Corrie, turning his head to look at her.

"*Gaoth,*" she said.

She wrote the word in the sand. *"Gaoth,"* she repeated. "It's my great-aunt's word. It's what she would say."

The word in the sand looked nothing like it sounded, Corrie thought.

"Gaoth, the wind. She is coming. She will blow hard tonight," said Kat stepping away from him.

He looked back to where she had pointed and saw again only grey on grey.

"If you're a visitor how come you speak like an islander?" asked Corrie hurrying to catch up with her.

"My family," she said, turning to face him but continuing to walk backwards in front of him. "My family's from the island." She twisted in a clumsy pirouette, her free arm gesturing to take in everything around her. "From here ... from Uig." She turned again so her back was once more to him. "Well, at least on my mother's side. My mother taught me to speak the tongue." She walked on. Corrie, weighed down and bent over with the heavy post, hirpled after her.

"She cannot tell a story without slipping into it," called Kat over her shoulder. "And the songs we sing are the songs she sang as a girl."

"What sort of stories?" Corrie asked.

"Just the usual. Selkies and water sprites ... you know."

Corrie didn't know. "What's a selkie?"

"You know ... a seal that's not really a seal." Kat looked out over the water again. "They're people really, dressed in sealskins. They come ashore sometimes, like seals do. Then they step out of their skins and dance on the beach. That's what a selkie is."

Kat did not slow her step and Corrie did not hear all the words that she spoke.

"Once there was a crofter who stole the skin of a beautiful selkie so that she couldn't return to the water. That was a bad thing to do, don't you think, to keep her a prisoner, to keep her from where she belonged? He came to a bad end and the selkie found her skin again and went back to the sea. Only there were children then, hers and the crofter's, and they weren't of the water or of the land. It's a sad tale, whichever way it's told."

"I see," said Corrie out of breath.

They walked on in silence.

They stopped to rest at the first of Corrie's pile of sticks.

"That you?" Kat nodded to the small collection.

"I didn't expect to find anything as large as this today," he said, indicating the heavy post he had let fall.

"You'd need a lot of those to keep a fire going," she scoffed, picking up one of the brittle white twigs, snapping it easily in two.

Corrie pointed to the trail of hedgehog mounds that led all the way back to the line of cottages. She laughed. Corrie laughed too.

"You just arrived?" said Kat, drawing her hair back from her face and tucking it behind her ear.

"Just arrived," he nodded.

"How long for?"

"Sounds like a prison sentence," he joked. "Same as you ... two weeks."

"Been before?"

"Lots. Every summer. Same two weeks. You?"

"Yes, every year, though we are earlier this year."

A wind was beginning to chop at the sea and the action of the waves was becoming more agitated. Corrie watched the curl of hair slip out from behind Kat's ear where she had tucked it and watched it fall flapping again across her cheek.

"We stay with my great-aunt. Perhaps you know her? She tends the sheep when she's not out on her boat. Red-haired. Oh … and she has a dog. Not really a pet, a work dog, always yelping. Bites at your feet if you're not careful."

"Sal," said Corrie, nodding again.

"That's it, Sal … short for Salute."

"Salute?" repeated Corrie.

Kat shrugged and held her elbows close to her body with the palms of her hands turned up. "Don't ask me," she said before Corrie could. "I just come with Mum," she went on.

"Mum … short for 'mumbo jumbo' perhaps," said Corrie, sniggering at his own attempt at a joke.

Kat did not laugh. She tried to brush the wisp of hair from her face but the wind flicked it back in place.

Corrie felt that he should apologise, though he was not quite sure for what. He turned away from her, kicking at the sand. With the swing of his leg he felt the weight of the found object in his pocket, felt it bounce against his thigh. He was reminded of something Kat had said.

"You said something before ... about Viking treasure," he said, trying but failing to hide the keenness of his interest.

"Eh?" she said, moving off again.

"Viking treasure in Uig, you said." He turned to see her walking away again.

He picked up the end of the heavy post once more and set off after her.

"Oh ... just another one of Mum's stories," said Kat, lengthening her stride and moving further from him.

"What story's that?" he called, his voice shredded and tossed away on the wind that was beginning to spin off the sea.

"Oh, you know ... stories of what was found here on the beach," Kat said, "buried in the sand. A cow stumbled over the treasure. That's what one story says."

"What was it?" urged Corrie. "What treasure?"

She seemed not to hear him. She pulled up the hood of her jacket and bent her head and her back against the buffeting blast. Corrie felt the whipping sting of sand on the side of his face and the cold slap of sea-spray as it lifted on the wind.

Kat turned to him and yelled something that was lost in the sudden moaning that was all about them. She turned back and quickened her movements, leaving Corrie trailing far behind her.

He gave up trying to catch her and slipped back into his own pace and into his own thoughts.

When at last he reached the foot of the drive that led to his cottage she was waiting for him, cowering behind the rough stone wall that gave some shelter from the weather. He almost didn't see her.

"You made it then," she shouted above the roar, tugging him down behind the wall by his sleeve.

Corrie dropped the heavy wooden post and crouched down beside her. It was quieter there. The howling wind seemed to pass over them creating a bubble of peace where they sat.

"I told you," said Kat, able to speak now without shouting.

"Told me?" said Corrie quizzically.

"*Gaoth*. I told you she was coming."

"*Gaoth* … the wind," said Corrie trying to copy the same strange guttural noise in the back of his throat.

He looked up towards the cottage. The car sat like the shell of some disembowelled beast, its four doors and boot open to the wind. The rain had started to slash the air. He saw his dad in an oversized yellow fisherman's mac run out of the cottage to lift one of the last boxes from the car

"I'd better go," said Corrie.

She held up the piece of the wooden post she had carried.

"Thanks," he said, taking it from her and standing up.

Kat grabbed his sleeve again, pulling him back into the shelter of the wall.

He looked into the gold-flecked, grey-blue of her eyes. She held his stare and did not speak.

"What is it?" he asked.

"When you share the found thing with me, I'll share more stories with you," she answered quickly. Then she sprinted away before he could think of a reply.

He stood up and looked after her. She was gone. He could not see her through the cold driving rain that pricked his cheeks and stung his eyes.

"Corrie!"

Hearing his dad's muffled call, he picked up the heavy piece of wood and lugged it up to the cottage door leaving a dark torn scar trailing behind him across the drive.

2. Gaoth

Corrie propped the wooden post up against the outside wall of the cottage and carried the shorter piece of wood into the small vestibule. Inside, it smelled familiar, damp and stale. They were always the first visitors of the summer. A lady from one of the neighbouring cottages aired the place the week before their arrival, dusted and hoovered the rooms, and freshened the sheets and blankets ready for their stay, but the smell never altered. Even at the end of their two weeks the smell was the same, though by then Corrie and his mother noticed it less. Corrie's dad, despite his heightened appreciation of the taste of Uig's air, never noticed it at all.

On the wall a little above his head were four crooked hooks with curling fingers. Corrie took off his jacket and hung it up. He reached his hand into the folds of wet material, patting the pocket that held the treasure.

"Get the door for me, Corrie," said his dad, brushing past him and disappearing into the house with the last of the boxes from the car.

Corrie snatched his hand back from his jacket and wheeled round guiltily, but his father was gone. He pushed the heavy front door shut. The wind chapped at the brass letter box flap. The rain beat a lunatic rhythm against the door. Corrie put the toe of one boot against the heel of the other and levered it loose. He then jerked his foot, kicking the loose boot into one corner of the stone-slabbed entrance hall. He repeated the action with his other foot.

"Is that you, Corr?" shouted his mother from the large room that served the cottage both as kitchen and dining room.

Corrie picked his way around the wet prints from his parents' shoes that trailed across the flagstone floor into the kitchen.

"Got some wood," said Corrie coming into the room and holding up the stubby splintered end of the wooden post. "There's more outside," he added.

His mother was kneeling in the fireplace, her head bent close to the grate as though she were praying before the altar of some strange spirit. She was nursing a thin flickering blue flame into crackling life. She looked up. A grey-black smudge of soot was smeared across one cheek. She smiled and nodded to Corrie, gesturing to the full basket beside the fire.

Corrie shrugged his shoulders and tossed his offering carelessly into the basket.

Corrie's dad was unpacking the contents of one box onto the old cracked wooden table in front of the window. Outside, a scowling grey had blotted out the sky, and the sea, churned into an angry snarling froth, pawed again and again at the white sandy beach. Wind and rain hurled against the front of the cottage, making a tap-tapping music against the windows, and howling down the chimney. Corrie's mother turned her face away from the fireplace coughing. The thin blue flame shrank, guttered and died.

"It's wild out there," said Corrie's father.

"Gaoth," said Corrie without thinking.

"What?" said his father turning to face him.

"Gaoth," said Corrie quietly. "It's Gaelic. It means wind or storm or something."

"Does it?" said his father. "Where did you learn that?"

Corrie hesitated. He did not want to tell them about Kat. They would persuade him to invite her over for tea one day. She would be a perfect holiday playmate for Corrie grinning at him out of every holiday snap. It happened all the time. His parents were always choosing friends for him.

"I read it somewhere," he lied.

"Blast!" cursed his mother getting up from her knees. "I think we'll have to use the electric fire tonight."

There was a perfectly good electric fire in the other downstairs room, the sitting room. Three bars — it heated the room up in no time. Corrie never understood why they didn't use it more often. It was more convenient and required a lot less work than the real fire ... and he wouldn't have to collect firewood every day.

Corrie picked his suitcase from the pile of boxes and bags behind the door.

"I'll just take this up to my room," he said, leaving his parents to sort out the heating problem. Shutting the door behind him, he put his suitcase at the foot of the stairs and nipped back into the vestibule. He pulled the found object out of his jacket pocket. It was still wet and a crusty covering of sand clung stubbornly to it. He brushed his hand across it and squinted at it, trying to see the coiled knotwork pattern.

Suddenly the kitchen door opened. Corrie froze. His mother stuck her head into the hall and called up the stairs. "Wash your hands, Corrie. Tea in five minutes." He was close enough to touch the back of her head. He held his breath and waited until she closed the door before racing over to his suitcase and rushing up the stairs to his room.

Corrie heaved the case onto his bed and, without even looking round at the room, took his find over to the window. The loose pane rattled in the wind. Corrie turned the found thing over and over in his hands, tilting it to catch the light. He knew where the pattern of coiled rope, or the twisted circle of snakes, should have been, but as hard as he tried he could not find the lightly raised, braided ring he had felt earlier.

He carried it over to the small sink that jutted out from the wall in one corner of the room and twisted on the tap. A hollow gurgling noise dribbled from the spout for some seconds, followed by a stuttering burst of water the colour of weak black coffee. Corrie drew back in surprise. He always forgot about the water. His father said it was the peat that gave it its colour, but to Corrie it just seemed dirty. They brought bottled water for drinking and for brushing their teeth, but they had to wash and bath in the brown brew that choked and spat from the taps. There was an electric immersion for heating the water, but it took a while for the tank to warm so that the water thrusting out of the tap now was cold. *As cold as water could be without being ice,* thought Corrie. He held the found thing between finger and thumb and tried to wash it without letting the water touch him. The sand slid off, collecting in the bowl of the sink, refusing to be washed away.

Corrie shook the drips from his treasure and carried it back to the window. It glistened, but there was still no sign of any markings. He lifted it to his ear and shook it gently, and then more firmly. There was no sound. He turned it over and pressed his thumbnail into the surface. His nail left a thin impression, no more.

"Corrie!" his mother shouted up the stairs.

Corrie turned back to the room. It was the same as it always was. The dark wooden bed pushed up against two walls, the shelves creaking with an assortment of books that looked like the books nobody buys. The shelves lined up on either side of the window, always in shadow. On one side of the bricked-up fireplace stood the sink with its mirror too high for Corrie to see himself.

"Corrie!" His mother's voice was anxious. He could hear her beginning to mount the stairs. He lifted the counterpane on the bed and looked underneath to see balls of fluff and a shiny black beetle, dead with its six bent-pin legs in the air. He slid the found thing into the shadows below, before dropping the cover back in place.

"Alright, Corr?" said his mother, knocking at the bedroom door.

"Coming," said Corrie, turning on the tap and pretending to wash his hands.

She opened the door but did not enter beyond pushing her head a little way into the room. She looked from the window to the bed and from the bed to the sink. She nodded and smiled at Corrie. "Just the same," she said.

"Always the same," muttered Corrie.

"Hungry?" said his mother.

"Starving," said Corrie, rushing past her and leaping down the stairs two at a time.

They sat one on each side of the table staring out at the wind and the rain. Tea was finished but no one had yet made a move to clear away the dishes. They were on holiday after all and life was allowed to trip along at a much slower pace. At home after tea Corrie would be drawn to the television where he would hope to be invisible until bedtime, at which moment he would remember that he had homework to do. On holiday there was no homework … and no television.

"Never expected this," said Corrie's father, nodding to the window.

"No," said his mother.

Neither were glum. For them it was all part of the adventure of being away from home.

"Be fine tomorrow, I expect," Corrie's father continued.

"Expect so," said his mother.

Corrie expected it to be just more of the same. He swung round in his chair and looked away from the window and into the room. The electric fire had been brought through from the other room and now sat in front of the real fire, its three bars glowing orange, giving off a thin, slightly unpleasant smell, like singed wool.

Corrie glanced up at the high mantelpiece. The carved wooden head he had found on the beach was still there. The black crack in its face had crept up into the shell-like curls of its hair, fading now from brown to a dull grey. Here and there the layers of paint had flaked away completely to reveal the bare wood beneath.

"It's so peaceful," said Corrie's father.

"What?" said his mother.

"Here. It's so peaceful here," he repeated.

"Apart from the storm, you mean?" laughed Corrie's mother.

"No. Even with the storm. Listen."

They listened.

It was true. Even with the storm outside moaning and whistling round the cottage, even with the letter box flapping there was a real peace in this place. Corrie craned his ears trying to hear what wasn't there to hear.

A sudden loud slap sounded from upstairs making them all start.

They looked up at the ceiling. The noise had come from Corrie's bedroom. No one spoke. They waited. Listening for a second noise.

Nothing happened.

"Probably just the wind," said Corrie's mother.

Corrie nodded.

"Better check though," his dad added, getting up to investigate.

He returned a few minutes later with a book in one hand. "Must have fallen off the shelves in your room, Corrie," he said, passing the book to him. It was a small, slim book with a hard grey-red cover, dusty and held together with brittle yellowing tape.

Corrie took the book. There was no writing on the cover and the spine was too broken to see. He blew the dust off the book and opened the first page. It was blank. He was just about to turn to the next page when a bright flash of lightning lit up the room, a blue-white light that bleached the colour from everything ... just for a moment. It was the briefest of moments, but in that time Corrie was startled by what he saw on the empty page. There was something lightly embossed in the centre. The lightning flash had picked it out in shadow — a braided ring coiled in an unbroken circle. *Snakes,* thought Corrie, bringing the book closer to his eyes.

A crashing roll of thunder shook the house and the lights flickered. "Are there any candles?" Corrie's mother wondered aloud. Her voice was raised a little and she sounded each word slowly and deliberately as if talking across a crowded room.

"I think we might need candles," she repeated.

A second flash of lightning brightened up the room. Corrie had the book at the wrong angle so this time it did not help. The lights in the cottage flickered once more and the electric fire crackled and sparked.

"Candles? Yes. Under the sink, I think," answered Corrie's father, looking out of the window up at the sky.

A second clap of thunder snapped and everyone jumped. It was as if the storm was in the room there with them. The air felt charged and the fine hairs on Corrie's arms stood up straight. He shivered.

When a third flash lit up the room, Corrie quickly covered his ears with his hands. The thunder sounded almost immediately.

"It's right above us now," said his dad.

The lights went out and the electric fire began making small clicking noises as the warm orange faded from the three bars. The room was dark. Corrie could see his parents silhouetted against the silvery grey of the storm-torn sky.

"You alright, Corrie?" asked his mother.

"Fine," said Corrie.

They listened to the rain, heavier now against the windows. Somewhere a choked gutter was spilling over, a ragged sheet of water falling to the ground with a constant splashing.

There was no more lightning. No more thunderclaps.

They waited, expecting more. The minutes ran into one another. Corrie could hear his own breath. No one moved. Still they waited in the lengthening stillness of the room.

"Passed over," pronounced Corrie's father at last, though there was uncertainty in his voice so that it was almost a question.

"Seems like it," said Corrie's mother. She, too, was uncertain.

"What about the lights?" said Corrie. "And the electric fire."

Corrie's father had moved from the table at the window and passed Corrie like a shadow into the cooking area. He was looking under the sink for the candles. "Early beds all round," he said cheerfully ... *too cheerfully,* Corrie thought. "Can't do much til the morning."

Corrie groaned.

"And it seems that there are no candles," his father added.

It was not easy getting ready for bed that night. Corrie got undressed in the near dark downstairs, keeping his socks on to protect his feet from the cold flagstone floor in the hall and the linoleum flooring in his bedroom. He had new pyjamas for his holiday. He always had new pyjamas for his holiday, every year. But tonight, no matter which way he fastened his pyjama jacket, he seemed to have at least one extra button, or one too few buttonholes.

"Keep your clothes in one pile, Corr," said his mother.

Corrie fumbled about, his arms reaching out in front of him, feeling for the clothes he had not kept in one pile. He ran his hand in a broad sweeping motion flat across the floor. He found the book with the embossed first page, but only some of his clothes. He tucked the book into the waistband of his pyjama trousers and gave up the search.

There was still a good deal of unpacking left to do and in the dark nobody could find the toothpaste or the soap.

"Just have to wash and brush twice in the morning," joked Corrie's dad.

"Yes," said Corrie's mother, not appreciating the joke.

Outside, the rain had slackened off but a thick wind still buffeted the cottage. When Corrie moved into the hall he could feel the cold draught playing through the house and, despite the socks, his feet nipped from the cold stone. He rose up onto his toes and took quick giant strides to the wooden stairs.

"Mind you close the shutters, Corrie," said his father, passing him on the stairs so quietly that Corrie leapt round in fright.

"Dad!" yelled Corrie, certain that his father had deliberately spooked him. It was the kind of game he played at home. His father was the only one who found it funny.

"Sorry … didn't mean to startle you," he answered. He sounded sincere but Corrie remained distrustful. "Just remember to close the shutters … keeps the draught out. Alright?"

"Goodnight," said Corrie, turning into his room.

He left the door half open and went to the window. The corner pane was rattling in the frame, just as it had for as long as Corrie could remember holidaying here. In the dark it was insistent and irritating. There was no moon tonight but he could see the foamy edge of the sea whipped into ghostly shapes by the wind lashing over the surface of the water. He pulled the shutters to and climbed onto the bed. There was no quilted downie like at home. Here, there were cold linen sheets and coarse woollen blankets tucked tightly under the mattress on either side and at the bottom, with a heavy counterpane draped over the top. Corrie put the book with the embossed first page under his pillow, eased himself between the crisp sheets and slid his body down until his head was under, trying by the warmth of his breath to heat the bed. Even through the sheets and blankets and with the shutters closed he could hear the irregular *clink-clinking* of the loose pane of glass, the wind pawing again and again at the outside of the house.

3. Awake

Something woke him ... some sound unfamiliar and close by. He listened in the blinding darkness, still half in sleep and not remembering for a moment where he was. It was quiet in the room. So very quiet. And cold. Corrie tried to turn over. The tightly tucked-in sheets and blankets pinned him to the bed as securely as if some heavy cord tied him down. The bedsprings complained with each shift in Corrie's weight, but gradually the sheets slackened their grip. He rolled over to face the wall, his back to the window. Disoriented by sleep and the darkness, Corrie could not tell where wall or window were. He continued to fidget in his new position. He twisted back until his body found again the warm hollow he had started in. The room settled back into the black silence that was so complete Corrie thought himself asleep. His eyes closed.

"Awake!"

It was a whisper, barely heard ... dreamt perhaps. He listened again. His own breathing was the only sound. He strained to hear the familiar clink, clinking of the loose pane. But it was quiet. No sound ... not even the wind sighing; not even the hushed hiss of the sea breaking over the sandy shore.

Corrie kept his eyes tightly shut, not trusting the darkness. He pressed his head into the pillow closing it over his ears. Now he could hear the beating of his own heart. It was not so much a drumming, but more a rushing sound, as if he was running as fast as he could to escape something.

"Awake!"

It was still only a whisper, but this time he heard it clearly, even through the pillow held firmly over his ears. He wanted to cry out. He thought he had, but the roaring of his own fear choked his scream.

He opened his eyes. The darkness closed round him. He sat up and looked about ... and saw only black night.

"She comes!"

The strange whisper sounded more in his own head than as if it came from somewhere in the room. He wondered if he *was* dreaming. It made no sense.

"She comes!"

Who comes? thought Corrie.

He wrestled back the bed covers and stepped down onto the floor. He still had his socks on but he could feel a gritty texture that had not been there when he had climbed into bed. It was sand; a thick scattering of sand at the very edge of his bed. Corrie, padded over to the window, feeling first for the bookshelves, then for the closed shutters.

"She comes at last!"

Corrie's fingers fumbled at the metal latch and he threw open the shutters. A thin, blue-grey light spilled into the room and the shadow of the window frame fell across his bed like a prison grille. Corrie looked at the floor. A trail of sand led from his feet back to the bed. Sticking out from underneath was the found thing from the beach, surrounded by a shining circle of sand. Corrie got down on his knees to look.

The sharp sand hurt his knees. He drew the found thing out from its ring of sand. It had split almost completely in two. Corrie lifted it onto his lap. As he did so he felt a thin rush of sand spill over his leg. He lifted the top half away and peered into the hollow inside.

"She comes at last!"

The voice was both in his head and at the same time in the thing staring up at him from its bed of sand within the box. It felt strange, like a dream … but also *not* like a dream. The sand cutting into his knees felt real enough. The cold linoleum floor was real too. But the found thing and the strange whispering voice seemed to slip beyond the real into somewhere else.

"Beware!"

Corrie shivered. Not a cold shiver, though he was certainly cold, his toes numb and aching. No, this shiver was a shiver of fear, a fearful anticipation that Corrie was on the edge of something terrifying and that the next step forward would drag him beyond the real into the somewhere else where the voice belonged … somewhere beyond the safe.

"Beware!"

Corrie got up and carried the bottom half of the box over to the window. By the faint light he was able to see the object inside a little more clearly. It was a small squat figure. White. Smooth. Like polished bone ... or ivory. Finely carved with its big round staring eyes that seemed, even in the dim light of Corrie's bedroom, just a little afraid. Corrie had never seen it before. He couldn't have ... it was old and belonged to an altogether other time. Yet there was something immediately familiar about the small figure: something Corrie recognised; something he *had* seen before.

He picked the figure carefully out of the box, as if it were alive. It fitted easily into the palm of his hand and felt warm, strangely warm, as if life did indeed rest in the small carved figure. Corrie felt its warmth spread through him, even reaching his toes so that the linoleum floor no longer bothered him. *Now this is a dream,* thought Corrie. *This sort of thing only happens in dreams.*

He tried hard to bring it all back to the real; to locate in his memory what was familiar about the figure, set it all into the context of the reasonable and the explicable. The grim-featured face stared back at him, the eyes searching his in an attempt to keep what was happening securely in the somewhere else.

Suddenly, the pane of glass clinked and a floorboard creaked on the landing outside Corrie's bedroom door.

"She comes!"

The window clinked again ... and again. Corrie

felt a draught enter the room through the open shutters. He listened, holding his breath, fighting back the panic that threatened to cloud his thought.

Outside the sea pawed again at the sandy shore, snarling and hissing like a spiteful cat. The wind barged again and again at the cottage walls. Downstairs the *flap-flap* of the letter box sounded like the impatient rapping of an unwelcome visitor.

There it was again; a groaning of wood, straining under the quiet tread of a heavy foot … just outside Corrie's door.

"She comes again!"

Corrie's fingers closed around the carved figure and he leapt for the safety of his bed, pulling the covers over his head to make himself invisible.

"She comes! Beware!"

The door opened.

Corrie screwed his eyes shut … and waited.

"You asleep, Corr?"

This time the voice was not in his head. It was real.

"Are you asleep, Corrie?"

It was his mother.

"Mmm?" said Corrie, pushing his head out from the bed covers.

"Wind's picking up again. We'll have to keep the shutters closed," said his mother. She seemed to float from the door to the window, ghost-like in her white nightdress. *In this shadowy light even the real seems dream-like and otherworldly,* he thought.

"For goodness sake, Corrie. What's this on the floor?"

Corrie could see his mum more clearly now, silhouetted against the light coming in at the window. He could just hear, too, the scrunch of her slippered feet on the spilled sand.

"What?" he asked.

"Sand!" said his mother.

"Sorry," said Corrie, sitting up in his bed.

"It's everywhere, Corrie."

"I found something on the beach, Mum." Just for a moment he wanted to tell her about Kat and the found thing. He wanted to show her the little carved figure still in his hand, let her touch it and feel its strange warmth, and then tell her about the voice. She would make sense of it all. She would make it safe again; safe and ordinary.

"What a mess!"

"Sorry."

She closed the shutters and fastened the heavy brass latch, throwing the room into darkness once again.

"You'll have to clear it up in the morning, alright?"

"Okay, Mum," said Corrie.

"Go to sleep now."

Corrie laid his head back on the pillow and shuffled snake-like until his shoulders were under the covers again. "Are the lights still out, Mum?" he asked quietly.

There was no reply. He lay still and listened. The broken window in his room clinked more emphatically now and downstairs the letter box was still rattling. He thought he could just make out the slow scuffing of his mother's slippers as she padded back to her bedroom, but he could not be sure. He strained to hear the door closing and the shifting of the springs as she slipped back into bed ... slipped back into sleep.

Corrie waited. Listening. He waited for the voice to return. But it did not. The wind set up a deep droning hum outside his window and drove the rain hard against the glass. In waves. Like the sea.

"*Gaoth,*" said Corrie quietly to himself. "The wind." *What was it Kat had said on the beach?* His eyes closed. "*Gaoth,* the wind. She is coming." *That was what she had said.* He wondered if Gaoth could be the same "she" that the voice had warned him of. "*She comes.*" He listened to the rain pitting at the window and the low growling moan of the wind. It was like an animal scratching to get in, clawing at the glass, again and again.

"*She comes again.*" the voice had said. It was raining again. Corrie's breathing slowed and his fingers loosened their grip on the small carved figure. The clinking window pane sounded softer, muted and distant. "*She comes again.*" Corrie turned on his side with his back to the shuttered window and let go of the piece of warm bone. "She comes at last. She comes at last. She comes at last," chanted his own inner voice over and over, like a mantra. It didn't make sense. "*She comes at last.*" It always rained in Uig. The voice didn't need to make sense. "*Beware!*" Corrie was asleep.

It was the sharp knocking at his bedroom door that woke Corrie the next morning. He heard his father thump down the last steps into the kitchen. Corrie opened his eyes. Thin needles of light pricked the blackness through the space where the shutters didn't quite meet.

Downstairs he could hear his father whistling and singing: whistling where he didn't know the words of the song and singing where he did. Something about a "summer holiday" and the "sun shining brightly." A pot lid clattered onto the floor and the singing broke off for a moment. Corrie heard his dad talking to himself. He thought about getting up, then decided against it. At least it was warm in his bed.

The singing started again. Another of his father's favourites. Belted out with all the tuneless enthusiasm of one just starting his holidays. "She'll be Coming Round the Mountain."

"She'll be riding on a push-bike when she comes," cut through the walls and rose up through the floor filling the house with noise. "She'll be riding on a push-bike when she comes." It wasn't that Corrie's father didn't know the right words. *This meant they'd be off on the annual cycle ride today,* Corrie thought, with bikes hired from the corner shop. As far as Corrie was concerned this was not a suitable subject for a song.

"She'll be riding on a push-bike, riding on a push-bike, riding on a push-bike when she comes."

This last line howled into a mock operatic finish.

Corrie sat up as if stung. "When she comes," he repeated, remembering the voice of the night

before. *"She comes,"* the voice had said. He leapt
out of bed, feeling the sand sharp beneath his feet;
proof that it hadn't simply been a dream. He began
tugging at the blankets and sheets. There was
nothing there; a dusting of sand where Corrie's
feet had rested, nothing more. Corrie tossed the
pillow to the floor revealing the book he had hidden the night before. He'd forgotten about the
book and its concealed ring of coiled snakes on the
first yellowing page. It didn't seem so interesting
now. He brushed it to one side. He was searching
for something much more important.

He began unwinding the top sheet from the
blankets, slowly and carefully. Nothing.

He tried to do the same with the first grey
blanket. It was considerably heavier than the
sheet and did not separate easily from the second
blanket. The more Corrie pulled the more they
clung together, as though they held a secret that
they could not give up. Corrie sank to his knees
and began patting the blankets with the flat of
his hands, slapping here and there, following no
particular order or plan, so that he searched some
folds twice and others not at all.

"It must be here somewhere," he muttered to
himself. It couldn't have been a dream. He lay flat
on the blankets on the floor and looked under the
bed. In the dark shadows he could see the dead
beetle and the balls of fluff. He also saw one half
of the found thing sitting in a broken ring of white
sand. He spun round to the window where the
other half of the box sat empty.

"It has to be here," said Corrie, returning to his

search with renewed enthusiasm. As he crawled over the blankets his knee leant heavily on a small hard object. Corrie trapped it with the cup of one hand and set about tracing a way to the object through the grey woollen cloth. Suddenly it was there, staring up at Corrie with its scared eyes.

He got to his feet with the carved figure face up in the palm of one hand, and moved near to the shuttered window. He lifted the brass latch and the shutters swung open with a drawn out groan. Corrie stepped back in fright, almost dropping the bone figure. The whole window was covered on the outside, etched in an interlacing criss-cross pattern of white through which only the sharpest pinpricks of light filtered. The marks were like scratches on the glass. Corrie thought of the brittle twigs he had collected on the beach the day before, like witches' fingers. He thought also of the curling hooks in the hall and how like fingers they had also looked, beckoning to him.

"She comes!"

It was the same voice as the night before. The same warning.

Corrie's fingers closed round the small bone figure, holding it tight, squeezing it hard, his knuckles white and straining. It grew warmer in his grip, warm like sun-burned stone, warm and hard. He could feel a pulse, as though it were alive. He could not tell if the pulse was his own or part of the carved bone figure. Almost as if he had wished it, the frost pattern dissolved. A fine white mist drifted away from the window, a thinning breath carried away on the morning's sea breeze.

Outside the day was bright and the light hurt Corrie's eyes so that he closed them tight.

He felt dizzy; light-headed and slightly sick. He stepped back and sat on the edge of the stripped bed. The bone in his hand was cool now. Corrie relaxed his grip and opened his fingers. In the full light of day he recognised the bone carving at once … the squatness, the staring eyes and the bullet shaped head. He had seen others a little like it in a glass case in the museum at home.

It had been a special exhibition. There had been more than a dozen bone figures, all part of a larger find that had been discovered in Uig a long time ago. Corrie and his parents had gone twice because of the connection with Uig. Knowing Uig had somehow granted them special status; a special familiarity, as if the carved figures belonged in part to them because they holidayed in Uig for two weeks each year.

Corrie held his breath. A chess piece … a bone chess piece. A single Lewis chessman like the ones discovered on Uig beach. *An important find,* he thought. He squinted closely at the carving trying to identify the piece. He remembered that the chess-piece kings and queens were seated figures, on finely carved chairs with armrests and high backs. The knights were clearly marked out too, sitting astride their equally squat ponies, their blunt lances tilted for battle. The bishops were easily spotted with their books clasped to their chests, their swirly crooks held upright and their bishop's mitres squarely on their heads. And there were other figures: soldiers with swords and shields, and crazed staring eyes, some with their bared teeth biting into the tops of their shields. All of them were different; similar ... but not the same. Individual.

Corrie decided that what he had must be a bishop, although the figure was without a distinctive mitre. Nevertheless, he was standing in a similar pose, with a staff of some sort held close to his body. At first, Corrie thought the figure was bald but closer inspection showed that his hair fell in four twisted braids from under a close fitting skull cap of some sort. Instead of a book, he held in his hand a bird with the same staring eyes and a short flame-leaved twig in its stubby beak. Corrie thought it might represent the bird from the Bible, the dove, the one Noah sent out from the Ark, which returned with an olive branch in its beak.

"You up yet, Corrie?" Corrie's father called up the stairs.

His first thought was to show his father what he had, to tell him everything. He would be able to explain it all ... the bone figure, the strange voice and the frost-twigs that had blocked his window then disappeared so suddenly. But Corrie remembered the wooden head he had found on the beach, which now sat on the mantelpiece out of his reach, the crack in its face deepening, blackening, the paint blistering and flaking. Corrie had thought it a real piece of treasure when he had brought it in off the sand. And his dad had agreed, suggesting that they would have to do some research to find out what ship it had once looked down from ... but they never did. Corrie had seen it fade from something bright and splendid to a piece of dull junk that cluttered the mantelpiece and gathered dust.

"Corrie?" called his father again.

"Coming," he yelled back, deciding to keep the bone chess-piece figure to himself for now. He pulled some of the books from one of the book shelves and stood the figure far back on the shelf and in shadow. Its frightened eyes stared back at him.

"I'll be back," said Corrie, not really knowing why he had said anything at all. Then he replaced the books so that the figure was hidden from sight.

Still in his pyjamas, Corrie went downstairs. His dad was standing in the flagstone-floored hall at the foot of the stairs. He was pulling on his over-sized yellow fisherman's mac.

"Just off to the shop, Corrie. Keep an eye on the breakfast for me. There's a good lad."

Corrie nodded.

"Just give it a stir. Stop it sticking to the pot." His father grinned and was gone, the front door shutting heavily behind him.

Corrie tip-toed across the cold stone floor into the kitchen. Two bars of the electric fire glowed orange and the air smelled only faintly now of burning wool. The table by the window was set for three. On the cooker at the other end of the room a pot of porridge steamed and bubbled with slow glooping noises.

"Porridge!" groaned Corrie.

His clothes were neatly folded on the arm of one of the chairs, together with soap and toothpaste, too, and a new toothbrush still in its packet. His dad had started the unpacking and also tidied up the room. Corrie didn't notice, just as he hadn't really noticed that the power was back on, or that, unusually, the real fire had not been lit.

"Porridge!" he groaned again and slumped into one of the armchairs.

4. Cat Got Your Tongue?

"Thought we'd all go for a cycle this morning," announced Corrie's dad. "I've hired the bikes. Jane says they'll need looking over first. Not been out since we used them last year!"

Corrie's parents laughed together, but Corrie wasn't listening. His head was bent over his breakfast and with the tip of his spoon he was poking at the porridge stuck to the bottom of his bowl, which had cooled and solidified into a rubbery lump.

"Jane says it will warm up this morning."

Jane was considered the font of all wisdom in Uig. Not least by Corrie's father who was always quoting her pronouncements on the weather. The reliability of Jane's weather forecasts was never doubted, despite the fact that they were founded on an unshakeable, stubborn optimism and were almost invariably wrong.

"Good," replied Corrie's mother. "We could do with a bit of sunshine this year."

"Jane says they had a scorching two weeks at the

beginning of May. She had to order in extra sun cream as it was so hot."

According to Jane they always had it good in May. It was entirely possible that her optimism even coloured her memory.

"Just leave it, Corr," whispered Corrie's mother, leaning across and putting his spoon down for him.

"Oh, Corrie ..." said his father, changing the subject, "... remember that old lady who loaned us her binoculars ... the year we went birdwatching?"

Corrie nodded and looked away out of the window. He did not really want to hear what his father said next.

"You know ... red-haired and with a great black staff. Looked after the sheep," said his father, not getting to the point. "She had a dog ... black and white ... and yappy."

"The one that always nipped your heels?" said Corrie's mother.

"Yes that's the one," said his father.

"Sal," said Corrie, still looking out of the window.

"Sal! That's right, Sal. Wow! How did you remember that?"

"Short for Salute," said Corrie.

"Really. Salute? Well, anyway, she died last week."

"What?" said Corrie, jerking round, suddenly interested.

"She was very old, Corrie. She told me once she'd been herding sheep here in the hills of Uig for more than seventy years. But that's not what

I wanted to say. Some of her family are up for the funeral. Jane says there's a great-niece who must be about your age. Katrine ... or Katrina, I think she said her name was ... or maybe it was Kathrine. Anyhow, she's bound to be a bit out of spirits so I thought you could ask her over or something. What do you say? Eh?"

"A great-niece?" said Corrie's mother.

"Yes, apparently they holiday in Uig every summer too. Though usually later than us ... or was it earlier, maybe?"

"And when's the funeral?" asked Corrie's mother.

"Tomorrow, I think, or the day after, but then they're staying on for a week or so, according to Jane."

"What do you say, Corrie?" said his mother, patting him on the arm.

"Mmm?" said Corrie, looking back out of the window.

"You'd be company for one another," said Corrie's father.

"Yes, company," echoed his mother.

Corrie did not reply. He was looking at the wall at the foot of the garden where he and Kat had sheltered from the wind and rain. She hadn't said anything about her great-aunt being dead. She hadn't seemed all that gloomy either.

"Your mum could make the first move for you, if you like?" said his father.

"Yes, I could do that."

"What do you say, Corrie, eh?"

Then there she was, on the other side of the

wall, almost as if he had willed her to be there. Her red hood was pulled up over her red hair, and she was grinning at him as if she knew they were talking about her. She waved him to come out before disappearing behind the wall.

"What's the matter, Corr? Cat got your tongue?"

"What?" said Corrie, pushing his chair back from the table and getting to his feet.

"Shall I ask her for you?" repeated his mother.

"Who?" said Corrie.

"Have you heard a single word we've said, Corrie? Goodness! It's little wonder that you …"

Corrie didn't hear the end of his father's speech. He rushed from the room, grabbed his coat, slid his feet into his boots and was shutting the door behind him as his mother shouted after him.

"Don't forget, Corrie. We're setting off on the bike ride about eleven!"

Corrie didn't hear that either.

Kat was waiting for him crouched down on the other side of the wall at the bottom of the garden, out of view of the house. Corrie ran down the drive, noticing the black drag mark he had made with the heavy fence post. Dark pink-red gravel chips showed on either side of the jagged black wound, like crooked teeth.

"Stay down!" hissed Corrie, coming round the wall and hunkering down beside her.

"And a good morning to you, too!"

"My parents!" said Corrie, making an apologetic face.

"Are you hiding me from them … or them from me?" said Kat.

"Hiding?" said Corrie defensively.

"Well, it's what you do, isn't it? Hide things."

Corrie looked away guiltily.

The wind had dropped to a slight breeze wafting in off a gentle sea that lapped at the shore in long drawn-out whispers. Above them, thinning trails of cloud floated across a blue sky that fulfilled all Jane's optimistic forecasting ... at least for the moment. Even the sun was up and the air already felt warm. Still Corrie doubted. If Jane had said it would be fine then it couldn't be. It was almost a law in Uig; one that only he recognised perhaps, but a law nevertheless.

"You hide things too," said Corrie at last.

"You mean my great-aunt?" said Kat.

Corrie nodded.

Keeping her head down Kat got up and made for the beach.

Corrie wished he hadn't said a thing. He got up and ran after her.

"Sorry," he said.

"What?" said Kat, with her hands deep in her jacket pockets and her shoulders hunched.

"I'm sorry about your great-aunt," said Corrie, looking back to see if his parents were watching from the window.

"That's okay," shrugged Kat. "She was a gruff old crow ... sometimes anyway. Who told you?"

"My dad was at the shop this morning," said Corrie.

Kat followed the line of driftwood and black bladderwrack that marked the storm's high tide. It was just the kind of morning to do some beachcombing. Aside from the plentiful supply of good firewood just waiting to be collected, storms usually left all kinds of treasure scattered on the sands. Corrie followed behind Kat, kicking at the dry seaweed, scanning for anything out of the ordinary. He dragged some of the bigger pieces of wood, washed up by the night's storm, further up the beach, in case he had to collect firewood later. Kat watched him without offering to help.

"It's good wood," said Corrie. He seemed to be always apologising to her.

"For the fire," nodded Kat.

"My daily chore."

Kat nodded again.

All the while she watched him, her eyes searching for his. Corrie felt uncomfortable under her gaze. He kept his face turned away, exaggerating the effort it was taking to move the driftwood.

"That was some storm last night," he said, out of breath.

"Said she'd come, didn't I? Said she would blow," said Kat.

Corrie brushed the sand from his hands and came level with Kat. "Yeah ... you did."

She was still watching him.

Corrie looked back at the cottage. "Power was out," he said.

"Did you open it then?" said Kat, knocking Corrie completely off guard.

"Open what?" he said pretending not to understand.

"The thing you dug out of the sand yesterday.

Did you open it?" she persisted.

"No ... I didn't open it," he said, speaking the truth. But though it was the truth, it sounded like a lie ... even to Corrie.

She was still looking at him ... waiting. Corrie could feel her eyes on his neck. He could feel her will to know stronger than his will to hide. He turned to face her.

"It opened itself," he said quietly.

The sea made a shushing sound, as though it was bidding them be quiet.

Still she waited, not speaking a word.

"Honestly ... it opened itself," Corrie said, throwing her a quick look. Her face was blank. "It just opened itself," he repeated.

"Probably cracked with drying out. What was inside?" Kat went on matter-of-factly.

"There was a voice, too," Corrie blurted out.

"What was inside?" Kat repeated.

"Didn't you hear what I said?" He wanted to tell her now all about the voice and the warning. It was important ... but she wouldn't listen.

"Was it empty or was there something inside?" said Kat.

"Sand!" said Corrie firmly. "It was packed full of sand!"

"And what was in the sand?" said Kat, seeing through the truth to the secret hidden in his words.

"If you know there was something in the sand, then maybe you don't need me to tell you what it was!" spat out Corrie.

"Don't be silly. How could I know that?" said

Kat. She sounded older when she spoke ... more grown-up.

"Do you know what Uig is famous for?" said Corrie, starting again, resolved to tell her everything.

"I don't like riddles," said Kat.

"Do you know?" insisted Corrie.

"It's famously dull most of the time," she replied glibly.

"Do you know about the chessmen?" said Corrie.

"What is this ... twenty questions?" asked Kat.

"They were found here ... on this beach," said Corrie.

"What were?" said Kat, losing patience.

"The chessmen; the Lewis chessmen! They were found here. In Uig!" said Corrie.

"I'm not much one for board games," said Kat. "You'll have to explain."

"You'd know them if you saw them. They're carved out of bone or something ... Little figures. Kings and queens, bishops and knights. Chess pieces. They're in museums now. I saw them in an exhibition."

"Chess pieces?" said Kat.

Corrie was not certain that he could remember all the details. "They're very old," he said. "Nearly a thousand years old, I think. They were found buried on this beach."

"Why would someone bury them?" asked Kat.

"I don't know," said Corrie.

Kat sighed, still not understanding where this was all leading.

"I don't know why. I don't think anyone knows

… not really. They were found maybe a hundred years ago, or more. I'm not sure when exactly … and now they're in museums."

"Someone buried an old chess set here on Uig beach? Someone else found it and now it's in a museum? So what?" said Kat.

"More than one chess set," Corrie corrected her. "Lots of pieces anyway. Like a miniature army; all carved and detailed. You must have seen pictures of them."

"Well, let's just say that I have but I don't remember. What about them?"

"I think I've found another one," said Corrie smiling, pleased with himself.

"Another chess set?" said Kat.

"No … not a set. A piece," he said, a little of the wind taken out of his sails for a moment.

"A single piece?" said Kat.

"Yes. It was in the sand … a bishop, I think," added Corrie.

"A bishop?" said Kat.

"Yes. And I think it spoke to me." Corrie looked away, unsure now he'd said it that he hadn't just dreamed the whole thing.

Kat kept silent.

"Did you hear what I said? I heard a voice. I think it spoke to me," said Corrie, pretending interest in something at his feet.

Still she didn't answer.

Corrie looked up and saw the sceptical arch of one of Kat's eyebrows. He turned away again.

"Maybe I just dreamed it," he said.

"What did it say?" she said at last.

"It doesn't matter. It was stupid really ... didn't make sense. I suppose dreams never do," said Corrie. "Not when you wake up, they don't."

Corrie stared back at the cottage. He did not see the arch of Kat's brow sharpen. If he had it might have given him the courage to tell her what the voice had said. He might have gone on to tell her of the strange heat in the bone figure; how the heat had spread through him so that he had not felt the cold of the linoleum floor. He might have told her, too, of the web of frost that had covered his bedroom window earlier that morning, before the bishop had made it all evaporate in a cloud of mist. But Corrie did not see her expression change

She looked him up and down, letting a little time pass, enough that Corrie began to relax.

"Can I see it?" she asked quietly.

"What?" Corrie replied, his eyes fixed again on the windows of the cottage.

"Can I see the chess piece that talked to you?" Kat repeated.

He couldn't decide if she was laughing at him or not.

Kat saw his back straighten and stiffen again.

"Well ...? Can I?"

Corrie shrugged evasively.

"I'd like to see it," she said.

He nodded. "It's in the cottage."

Kat sat down on the sand, facing the sea. Corrie poked at a clump of seaweed. Black and dry on the top, underneath it was a shiny green-brown. He bent down, pushing it to one side. A white stone lay half buried in the sand. It was thick at one end and came to a point at the other. Corrie picked it up and turned it over and over in his hand. It was not glassy like crystal, but like hard chalk; pitted at the thick end with an unmarked clean surface at the other. He held it out to Kat.

She looked up at him, smiled, then took the stone and examined it. She knew it was a gift and also knew that she had to give something in return.

"Fiacail dràgoin."

"What?" said Corrie.

"It's a dragon's tooth!" she exclaimed.

Corrie laughed.

"No, really…," said Kat. "I've seen one before."

"It's a stone," said Corrie, still laughing.

"Yes, it *looks* like a stone," said Kat, trying to keep a serious face.

"It *is* a stone," said Corrie.

"It's a dragon's tooth. Very old. Probably fossilized. That's it … a fossilized dragon's tooth," said Kat.

Corrie decided to play along.

"I see," he said frowning, scratching his chin and nodding at the same time.

"Yes, yes. This rough end is where the tooth was fixed to the dragon's gum," said Kat, enjoying herself.

"Oh, I get it," said Corrie in mock earnest, still frowning and scratching and nodding.

"And this smoother, thinner and sharper end is the tooth itself. Perfect for tearing into …"

"… the skin of young princesses sacrificed to appease the beast's hunger," Corrie continued without expression, as though reciting a scientific principle or formula.

The lap-lapping of the sea on the sand was suddenly sharper. Corrie sat down next to Kat.

"My mum found a stone like this once," said Kat.

"Really?" said Corrie, recognising the end of the game.

"Really," said Kat. "On this beach ... a stone just like this one."

"And she called it a dragon's tooth?"

"*Fiacail dràgoin,* yes," laughed Kat. "She tells a great story about a dragon too."

"What, a fire-breathing, bat-winged thing guarding a great treasure of gold and stuff?" said Corrie, settled now on the sand beside Kat.

"No, nothing like that. This was a sea dragon," said Kat holding the stone up to the light.

"A sea dragon? You mean like a sea serpent?" said Corrie.

"Sort of, I suppose. It came out of the sea and when it left the island it went back to the sea," said Kat.

"So, it's a local story?" said Corrie.

Kat shrugged. "She's always telling stories. 'Passing them on' she says."

She rubbed the ball of her thumb over the point of the "dragon's tooth" stone. It didn't feel sharp enough to rip anything. "Anyway ...," said Kat, proceeding to tell Corrie the story in her mother's own words, for Kat had heard the story told many times. And as she told it, she seemed to Corrie to become much older than she really was and her voice did not seem like her own.

"Long ago a sea dragon rose up out of the sea and on the back of a great wind she came to the island."

"Why is it always 'long ago' and where have all the dragons of long ago gone?"

Kat scowled at him to hold his tongue. "That's how it's told," she said. "That's how my mother tells it." Then she continued with her story: "The people saw her coming from a long way off but they didn't know what it was. If they had they'd have left their homes and all they owned and climbed into their small boats and sailed away. It was a great creature with an enormous tail and sharp slashing claws that could rip a village from its roots with a single swipe." Kat clawed the air with a sweep of her hand. "Her teeth were as sharp as ice and her breath as cruel and cold as frost. She rose up out of the sea and coiled herself around the island ... three times ... and the island was wrapped in a never-ending winter. No one could escape. Food became scarce and the islanders fell sick. All the trees were cut down, whole forests laid flat; cut down for the fires that were the only protection against the biting cold. When the wells froze as hard as rock and the people's prayers froze on their frost-bitten lips, the hope in their hearts cracked and splintered like jagged shards of glass or cold ice. All seemed lost ... but it wasn't."

"It never is in stories," said Corrie, filling in the dramatic pause that Kat had allowed.

She ignored him and continued, telling it as she had learned it at her mother's knee, using her mother's words. "A small fishing boat had been anchored a little way from the island when the sea dragon had crawled up out of the sea. A small rowing boat it was. When the fisherman saw the sea dragon wrap herself three times round the island he put his arms to the oars of his boat and rowed away from there, rowing for many days without rest; rowed and rowed though his back ached and his hands blistered and bled. Rowed and rowed and rowed, until he reached a kingdom far to the north where a powerful golden-haired king ruled. A king with a fierce army of warrior giants, whose tramping feet made the earth shake and tremble. An army so fierce and fearless that there was none better in the whole world.

"The fisherman told the king about the sea dragon and asked for his help. Now the king had no reason to help the fisherman or the people on the fisherman's island. He owed them no favours and they had nothing with which to pay him and his warriors, but he was a king who valued courage and strength above all the plundered jewels in his kingdom, and he could see that the fisherman was courageous and strong. So he gave the fisherman one of his ships and a crew to sail it and sent him back to the island in the company of one of his wise men. After many days they reached the island and could see the coils of the sea dragon, half in and half out of the water, the dragon sleeping under a freezing blanket of mist. Even the hardened faces of the warrior crew grew pale and the fisherman fell to his knees and cried. The wise man stepped up to the front of the boat and poured into the sea a foul-smelling potion he had mixed. At once the sea began to bubble and boil as though heated by a great fire that spread around the island.

"The sea dragon woke from its sleep; its anger sounding as an icy blast across the island and it lifted its head and looked down on the small ship. The beast loosened its great coils and thrashed the sea with its tail sending forth a mighty storm that tossed and turned the ship about, but the wise man beat on the water with a stick and stilled the storm. The creature's anger swelled. It took a great breath and blew down on the ship so that a fierce and bitter wind chilled the bones of the giant warriors and froze the oars in their hands and snapped the ropes and split the sails as sharply as I might break a dry twig. There was a cry from the island; a woman's cry. But the wise man only breathed into the cup of his clasped hands and, when he opened them again, a silver-feathered bird rose up and flew about the ship trailing at its tail a warm draught that thawed the frost and calmed the wind. The sea dragon's cold fury erupted. It broke its teeth on the hard rocks and blunted its claws on the iron-hard earth. It was the sea dragon that clawed the bay here at Uig; scooped a great dent in the land that the cold sea rushed to fill. It would have torn the whole island into a ragged scatter of rocks had not the wise man called up to the beast.

The creature bent close to see more clearly this man, so small and strangely powerful; bent close enough to fix the wise man with the cold green stare of its eyes. Close enough that the flaring of its great nostrils cut a chill stinging whip of air across the ship. Close enough and then too close.

There was a another cry from the island and the wise man took up the stick that had beat the storm still and now set it to beat the sea dragon. So sorely did the stick thrash about its head that the pained screams of the serpent carried to the far corners of the world, and all who heard them shivered and drew nearer their warm home fires. Then suddenly the sea dragon uncoiled itself from the island and shrank back hissing and spitting into the boiling sea."

Kat stopped, staring out to the farthest reach of the sea.

"And was never seen again," said Corrie following where she looked.

Kat held the "dragon's tooth" stone tightly in her hand.

"Why did the dragon come to the island in the first place?" Corrie asked at last.

Kat shrugged.

"There must have been a reason?"

"Some things just happen," Kat replied.

"Not in stories ... in stories things happen for a reason."

Kat shrugged again.

Corrie could see that she was lost in thought, not really listening to what he was saying. He noted the tight grip she had on the dragon's tooth stone.

"So, afterwards ... where did the dragon go?"

"Back where it came from, I suppose," said Kat.

"Then what's to stop it coming again?"

"Don't ruin it," she cautioned him. "It's my

mother's story, one that she has told me since I was young. My great-aunt told it to her when she was a child."

Corrie hadn't been trying to spoil it. He wanted to say he was sorry.

"It's a good story," said Corrie.

"Just a story," said Kat, her voice her own again. She shifted her gaze from the horizon to the stone in her hand. "Just a story."

"What do you suppose happened to the magician?" said Corrie.

Kat shook her head. She looked up. "Could be still here for all I know ... waiting til she comes again."

Corrie felt a sudden cold breath on the back of his neck. He shivered. "You said 'she?'" he said.

"The sea dragon," said Kat. "Returning on the back of another great wind."

Corrie felt a creeping coldness spread through him. He wanted to tell Kat about the voice and its warning. It seemed important. Somehow it seemed linked to the story she had told, though he could not say how. He struggled to make connections that just wouldn't fit, like pieces of a badly cut jigsaw, or like images in a dream whose edges dissolve on waking. He wanted to tell her everything, but his lips stayed shut, as though frozen.

"It's just a story," laughed Kat, getting up to go.

Corrie cupped his hands together and breathed into them, rubbing the warmth into his fingers.

"So will you show me it?" she asked, brushing the sand from her legs.

Corrie opened his hands. They were empty.

"The chess piece ..." said Kat. "Will you show it to me?"

Corrie inclined his head, still unable to speak.

Kat nodded back. She turned and ran off in the direction of the cottages. Corrie watched her go. Her run was awkward on the beach, her feet slithering in the uneven sand. She stopped when she reached the road and turned back to face him.

"Thanks," she called, gesturing to the "dragon's tooth" stone and put it into her jacket pocket.

Corrie shrugged. "It's just a stone," he said, so quietly that she did not hear, so quietly that it was like a lie.

The sea lifted and fell, slow, unravelling like torn lace at its edge. And at the edges of his thoughts too, something was unravelling.

5. A Little Magic

The annual bike ride did not go ahead as planned. The day turned colder, despite Jane's prediction for warmth. Wind and rain kept them all inside for much of the day. They played cards in front of the electric bar fire, or read books, or sat doing nothing, and pretended that this was what holidays were really about ... at least Corrie was pretending.

Sometimes Corrie's gaze wandered to the window, and further, looking for the red of Kat's jacket beyond the wall of the garden. He thought again and again of the story she had told. He thought of the chess piece and the voice he had heard or maybe imagined. He thought of sun and blue skies and the holiday photographs his friends would show him at the end of their summer.

That night Corrie dreamed the voice again. The same message, waking him out of sleep.

"She comes."

Corrie lay as still as still, listening to the talking dark.

"Beware. She comes." That was all the voice said. *"Beware. She comes."*

Corrie stayed silent.

The next morning they set off early, just as soon as Corrie's father had collected all three bikes from Jane's, pumped up the soft tyres and oiled the dry chains. They took a packed lunch and headed off down the coast road ... the only road ... the same road.

"It's a good enough day. We might try a little further this year," said Corrie's father.

They always started off with the same bluff confidence. Even the year it had rained so hard that it had been like cycling through a stream and they had got no further than the first bend before they had had to turn back utterly soaked.

"Not too far, Dad, eh?" said Corrie, anxious to get back and show Kat the bone chess piece.

Corrie's father laughed and set off, leading the way. Corrie followed next, his mother bringing up the rear. Despite having been "looked over", the bikes all squeaked and rattled as much as they ever did.

"Taste that air!" called Corrie's father over his shoulder.

Corrie sighed and switched off.

The day before, after Kat had left the beach, Corrie had at first gone back to the cottage and up to his bedroom. His mother had already remade the bed and swept the floor clean of sand. The two separated halves of the found thing sat on the windowsill. Empty. The book with the hidden ring of braid lay open on his pillow. Corrie pulled some of the books from the shelves until he found the carved bone figure sitting in the shadows. Then, he had lifted it carefully into the light and re-examined it. The fact that there was no bishop's mitre on its head bothered him. He tried to see where the curling crook of its bishop's staff was broken, but the top of the staff was rounded and smooth. In fact, the more he looked at it the less like a bishop it looked. And what about the bird in his raised hand? Corrie thought of Kat's wise magician and the silver-feathered bird ... the warmth it had trailed at its tail.

Then Corrie noticed something that made him start, something he had not noticed before. Round the hem of the figure's gown was carved a decorative band; a band of braid that twisted in and around itself. But it was not a simple braid. At the front of the gown the pattern ended with a head. The head of a stylized beast, with beady eyes, jagged teeth and exaggerated nostrils. In its teeth it held the other end of the braided ring so that the circle was unbroken. And this other end was shaped into a pointed tail, like a snake's tail ... like a sea dragon's tail. At least like the tail that Corrie had imagined when Kat had told the story of the sea dragon coiled three times around the island.

Corrie had wrapped the figure in a clean handkerchief and smuggled it into his jacket pocket before his dad came back with the three bikes.

"See that, Corrie?" said his father pointing excitedly towards the almost purple hills.

"What?" said Corrie, interrupting his thoughts and returning to the rattle and squeak of the three bikes.

"Over there. See it?"

Corrie looked to where his father pointed.

"A lapwing!" said his father.

The lapwing hung a moment in the air and then fell. They saw it perform a series of acrobatic tumbles: rising and falling in untidy arcs and loops through the air; rolling from side to side, screaming a loud agitated *pee-wit* on every rise.

"Yeah ... I see it," said Corrie, unable to pretend the same interest and excitement as his father.

A second bird took to the air and the two lapwings twisted and turned in an impressive display of aerial gymnastics. Stopping the bikes in the next passing place, they sat back to watch. Corrie's mother had fallen a little way behind.

"We should have brought your binoculars out with us," his father said.

"Mmm ...," Corrie replied, glad that they had not yet been unpacked.

"Next time, eh?" said his father.

"Mmm," Corrie said, non-committally.

Corrie could tell that his father was about to reminisce about their time bird-watching in the hills with Kat's great-aunt's borrowed binoculars.

"Dad?" he said, intent on steering the conversation down a different path. "Dad, do you remember that exhibition we went to see a couple of years back?"

"What exhibition was that, Corrie?"

As if they went to exhibitions on a regular basis,

scoffed Corrie. He couldn't recall having been to any other ... before or since.

"The one about the chessmen," he said.

"Oh yes ... I remember that. Didn't we go to see that exhibition twice?"

"Yes ... that's the one!" said Corrie.

"The Lewis Chessmen. That was it. They were found on the beach at Uig, you know."

"Yes ...," said Corrie, "I know."

At that point Corrie's mother pulled into the passing place, out of breath, pink-cheeked and grinning. Corrie's father pointed to where the two lapwings wove their crazy cartwheel patterns in the air.

"Lapwings!" she said. Even Corrie's mother had been infected by their previous interest ... enough to know some of the more obvious birds at least.

They watched in silence, waiting for Corrie's mother to catch her breath.

"Wonderful!" she said. "We should have brought your binoculars."

"Next time," said Corrie.

"Yes. Corrie was just remembering that exhibition we went to see," said Corrie's father. "The one about the chessmen."

"The chessmen? Oh ... the ones from Uig? Yes I remember that. We went twice, didn't we?" said Corrie's mother.

"What were they made of?" asked Corrie.

"Oh, bone or ivory, I should expect," said his father.

"Walrus ivory," said his mother, "... carved from walrus tusks."

"Oh yes … you're right. I remember now. Walrus tusks," said his father.

"Where did they come from?" said Corrie.

"What? The walruses or the chess pieces?" said his mother.

"The chessmen," said Corrie.

"Why the interest?" said Corrie's father. "You didn't show this much interest when we went to the exhibition?"

"How did they get here?" asked Corrie.

"You've stumped me there. What does the expert say?" Corrie's father indicated his mother.

"I don't know about being an expert," his mother laughed.

"Go on, Mum."

"Well, Corrie. I don't think anyone really knows for certain. Some think they were made in a workshop in Norway. I don't know if that makes them Viking or not. But they were probably brought here for trade and somehow ended up buried on the beach."

"And were they just regular chess pieces?" asked Corrie.

"I don't know if you would describe them as regular. There were kings and queens."

"And bishops and knights on horseback," said Corrie's father.

"Yes, I think so. I liked the knights on the horses. They were quite cute really. The horses were like snub-nosed Shetland ponies," said Corrie's mother.

"I remember the soldiers with their teeth gnawing at the tops of their shields … wide-eyed, like crazy men," said his father.

"'Bezerkers' I think they were," added his mother. "Soldiers made wide eyed and crazy for battle. I read somewhere that the warriors drank an intoxicating liquor that gave them courage and great strength, and made them mad for blood."

"But were there any other kinds of figures?" pressed Corrie.

"What other chess pieces are there?" said his mother.

"Pawns," said his father, "but they were just pieces of bone ... shaped like small gravestones, if I remember rightly."

"But no other figures?" said Corrie. In his jacket pocket, his fingers gripped the hankie-wrapped figure. Through the cloth he could feel it begin to grow warm, suddenly.

"I don't know what you mean," said his father. "That's a complete chess set. What else could there be?"

Corrie shrugged.

"Maybe there's a book about them in the cottage," said his mother.

"A book?" said Corrie.

"Well, there're lots of old guide books and books about the island. The chessmen are bound to be mentioned in one of them, I would think."

Of course, thought Corrie, *the book*. He had been so preoccupied with the chess-piece figure that he hadn't even looked inside the book yet.

"Shall we press on then?" said Corrie's father, swinging his bike round towards the road.

Corrie didn't want to "press on." He tightened his grip on the carved ivory figure in his pocket and wished that he didn't have to go any further. He wasn't altogether sure why he did that. Maybe it was that wishing for the frost fingers to be gone from his window the day before had seemed to have been a wish granted by the chess piece in his hand.

"I think I'll just wait here," said Corrie's mother. "Feeling a bit numb already."

"Corrie?"

"Oh. I'll just wait with Mum. You go on, Dad," said Corrie.

"No, don't worry about me, Corr. You can go with your dad. I'll be fine."

The warmth of the figure spread through Corrie, like before.

"No, really, Mum. I hurt my leg back there anyway." And though it was a lie, Corrie was able to show his mother an oily mark on the bottom of his jeans where the chain had rubbed against his leg.

"Well, save me some of that picnic," said his father, moving out of the passing place and onto the road. And strangely, as his father drew away, Corrie felt the warm figure, still in his hand, begin to cool.

On the journey back they had to dismount about a mile from the cottage. Corrie's mother could not pedal any further and Corrie's father eagerly accepted this as reason enough to give up on the wheels. So, they walked the last mile.

Corrie might have enjoyed a private gloat. They *had* overdone it, as they always did ... as Corrie had known they would. He might have inwardly cheered for they would not cycle again this summer. He might even have teased his parents for their lack of fitness, or joked with them about the lumpiness of the saddles on the old bikes. But Corrie's mind was elsewhere, running ahead of him, opening the cottage door and leaping up the stairs to his bedroom, snatching the book that still lay open on his pillow, and turning the pages. *And all would be revealed,* he thought.

On reaching the cottage, Corrie's father took Corrie's bike and carried on up to Jane's. His mother leaned hers against the wall and limped to the front door. Corrie was ahead of her, running, pushing open the cottage door, stopping only to kick off his boots before leaping up the stairs to his bedroom and snatching the book from the pillow. All with the dream-like sensation of déjà vu.

He flicked through the pages. They were stiff and brittle with age. The yellowed Sellotape that held the book together cracked and crumbled, allowing the loosened pages to slide away from each other. Corrie leafed impatiently through the book, certain that it contained something that would link it with the ivory figure in his pocket. The book had no pictures ... just text. Even that was no good to Corrie for it was written in a different language.

So desperate for a connection was he that he continued to rifle through the pages not minding that the unnumbered sheets slipped free and floated this way and that, caught in the draught that had found its way through Corrie's open bedroom door.

Then something registered. There it was ... a

connection … a single word, printed in bold type. A chapter heading. A tenuous link perhaps … but in Corrie's mind definitely a link.

He traced a line with his finger under the word. He recognised it. It was what Kat had written in the sand.

"Gaoth," he read out loud.

So the book was in Gaelic. That meant it could be deciphered or translated. *Kat could probably do it,* he thought, staring hard at the lines of type hoping beyond hope that some meaning would leak into his consciousness … but the words lay flat. The strange configurations of letters refused to give up their secrets … at least to Corrie.

The front door shut with a dull wooden thump and a last gasp of cold air breathed into Corrie's bedroom. The loose pages on the floor lifted like dry leaves and drifted away from the door, settling around Corrie's feet. He got down on his knees and collected the pages together. They were out of sequence and Corrie, because he could not determine their order, simply slipped them between the hard covers of the book and shut the book tightly so that they could not escape again.

Again the weather turned chill and the wind punchy. Corrie was restless. He had things he wanted to tell Kat. He'd promised to show her the figure and now there was the book.

"You alright, Corrie?" his mum said.

He didn't hear at first. He was at the window

again. The rain on the glass made the view dissolve and shift, colours running into each other and the colours mostly grey.

"Corrie?"

He heard his name and turned to his mum.

"You seem very far away. Is everything alright?"

"Tired, I expect," laughed Corrie's dad. "We cycled quite far today."

They hadn't, but Corrie agreed that that must be it.

His sleep was broken again. The same voice, the same words as before.

"She comes. Beware."

A little louder perhaps, Corrie thought, and that was the only difference.

After breakfast the next morning, Corrie put the book into his pocket, next to the figure, tugging the zip on the pocket closed as far as it would until it snagged on one of the tiny crooked metal teeth. Then he leaped back down the stairs, pulled on his boots and was running back down the gravel drive when his mother called out after him, "We need some more wood for the fire, Corrie!"

He did not stop to listen, but hurried onto the road, back towards Kat's great-aunt's house, meeting his dad returning from the shop with Jane's daily weather forecast. "What? You've still got energy enough to run?" said his father, pretending to rub at an ache in his back.

Corrie waved and ran on without stopping. He didn't want to explain where he was going, nor about Kat and the book … and everything else. He ran past his father and kept on running until he neared the first house. He looked back to check if his father was watching.

Reassured by the square slope of his father's back, Corrie unzipped his pocket and took out the carved figure still concealed in his handkerchief, before approaching the small wooden gate. The latch was broken, the gate held shut with a loop of blue plastic. Corrie let the gate swing away from him, squealing on its rusted hinges.

Suddenly Sal was there, rushing towards Corrie, barking wildly. Corrie could not move. He gripped the bone figure tightly in front of him, closed his eyes and wished that Sal would not nip his heels or any other part of him. And just as before, Corrie felt the ivory chess piece grow warm in his hand. The barking continued but came no closer.

Corrie opened his eyes. Sal was straining to reach him but failing, prevented from getting any closer to him by a blue plastic cord that was fastened to his leather collar. Corrie felt the figure cool again.

A window in the cottage opened and a woman leaned out and shouted at Sal to be quiet. Sal stopped at once, his tail between his legs, body low to the ground as he slunk away out of sight down the side of the cottage.

The woman turned to Corrie and looked him up and down, waiting for him to speak. Her faded red hair was tied back from her face and there was something he recognised in the way she looked him up and down. It was just as Kat had done when they had met on the beach that first day.

"Em ... I'm looking for Kat," said Corrie.

"Katrine?" said the woman sharply.

"Yes, sorry ... Katrine," said Corrie. *Now he was apologising to Kat's mother,* he thought, *just as he had apologised to Kat.*

The woman continued to stare at him. She had the same hard gaze as her daughter, though the eyes were red rimmed and the skin around them creased with the years.

"Is she in?" asked Corrie.

The woman shook her head.

He was about to go when the woman spoke again. "You Corrie?" she asked.

Corrie nodded. Kat must have talked about him to her. He was pleased and smiled up at the woman.

"Was it you who found the *fiacail dràgoin* yesterday morning?" she asked.

"What?"

"The dragon's tooth."

"Yes. Kat ... I mean Katrine ... told me the story," said Corrie.

"The sea dragon," said the woman, nodding gravely.

"Yes," said Corrie.

They faced each other in silence again. Corrie wasn't sure if the conversation had ended. He felt that it would be impolite for him to just turn and go. At the same time he felt awkward staying.

"I'm sorry about Katrine's great-aunt," he ventured.

The woman bowed her head in acceptance, but said nothing.

Corrie looked away. It was harder than ever to go, yet even more uncomfortable to stay. He looked down at the hankie in his hand with the figure still inside. He thought about making another wish, but the words wouldn't form. He gripped the figure tightly willing it to grow warm again, but it remained cold and hard in his hand. He looked up at the woman still at the window.

"If you wait long enough she will come," said the woman at last.

"Sorry?" said Corrie, not sure that he had heard right.

"She will come," repeated the woman.

"Katrine …?" said Corrie, thinking she must be talking about her daughter. "Do you mean Katrine?"

"Katrine is on the beach, where she always is," said the woman. "You can wait and she will come, or you can go to her." And she turned back into the room, pulling the window shut before Corrie could fully take in what had been said.

6. Beyond Reasonable Doubt

It was cold on the beach. The morning sun with all of Jane's usual optimistic promise had given way to scowling cloud, great rolling banks of it moving in off the sea, brooding and dark. Corrie fastened his coat shut.

"Summer!" he scoffed.

He looked back at Kat's great-aunt's cottage. A thin smudge of smoke rose in a slow spiral from the blackened chimney and hung in the air above the cottage. Corrie thought he saw some movement at the drawn curtains, but he couldn't be certain.

He turned back to the beach and set off along the sand, past the line of cottages with their blank, staring windows looking out to sea.

She will come. That's what Kat's mother had said to him. *She will come.*

He heard Kat call his name. At least he thought she must have called for he looked up and saw her waving to him. Corrie waved back and quickened his pace, stumbling into a run that soon tired and slipped back into a walk.

Kat stayed where she was, waiting. Corrie could feel her watching him. He offered up a broad and exaggerated smile hoping she could see it.

"Have you got it?" she called when Corrie was still a little way off.

Without slowing his pace he held up the ivory figure, still hidden in the handkerchief and nodded.

"Where's the bishop, then?" she said as he came level with her.

"I've got it. Only I don't think it's a bishop anymore," said Corrie unable to hide his excitement.

"What is it then?"

"I don't know." He unwrapped the ivory carving.

Kat leaned close and examined the figure without touching it.

"See? There's no mitre," said Corrie.

"What?"

"Mitre ... the hat that bishops wear," he explained.

"I know what a mitre is," she snapped.

"Well, it doesn't have one and other bishop chess pieces do. This one's different. And ... it doesn't carry a crosier like the others."

"Crosier." The word surprised even Corrie. He must have heard the word before ... or read it at least — probably at the chess-piece exhibition — but it was not a word he had ever used before, nor one he could even remember hearing or reading. It seemed to have come from somewhere deep and hidden, without his effort. Corrie understood that words could do that sometimes, but he felt sure that the word was not his but someone else's. He also knew that it was the right word, but did not know how he knew that.

"He's just carrying a plain staff," said Corrie.

"It's sort of familiar," said Kat.

"I told you you'd recognise it. It's like the other chess pieces," said Corrie. "But not," he added.

"What do you mean?" said Kat.

"Do you see the bird in his hand?"

Kat looked closely and then nodded.

"Well, at first I thought that was like the dove that was sent out from the Ark. Like in the Bible ... you know ... the one sent out from the Ark that returned with an olive branch as proof that the flood was over. That's why I thought it was a bishop, or at least a holy man."

Kat nodded again.

"But, like I said, it's missing a mitre and a bishop's staff ... so it can't be a bishop," said Corrie.

"Noah."

"What?" said Corrie.

"It must be Noah," said Kat.

"But there isn't any Noah in chess," said Corrie.

"But I thought you were saying that it wasn't a chess piece. Like a chess piece and not, you said."

"Well ... yes. But it isn't Noah," said Corrie.

Kat shrugged. "If it's not a bishop and it's not Noah, then what or who is it?" she said.

"Take it a minute." Corrie held the figure out to her.

Kat grasped it pinched between finger and thumb.

"Listen," said Corrie. "Remember I said there was a voice too?"

"The one you dreamed?" said Kat holding the figure up close to her nose.

"Yes. Only I don't think I dreamed it. I know I said that, but it was *real*. It is real. Every night I hear it in the same way and saying the same thing," said Corrie.

This time he *saw* the arch of Kat's eyebrow and read in it all her unspoken scepticism.

"I know ..." he said. "It doesn't make sense to me either."

"Go on," she said, lowering the figure and giving Corrie her full attention. "What does it say ... the voice?"

"It warns me about something. It keeps repeating 'beware' and 'she will come.'"

"Who will come?" said Kat.

"I don't know," said Corrie.

She pretended to re-examine the figure, deliberately not looking at Corrie, but all the while waiting for him to continue.

"Look," he began again. "Grip the figure tightly in your hand."

She did as he instructed.

"Right," he asked, "What does it feel like?"

She shrugged not understanding what it was he wanted her to say.

"Just describe what it feels like," said Corrie.

"It's hard," she said uncertainly.

He nodded encouragement.

"Hard like stone," she said.

He nodded some more.

She closed her eyes and tightened and loosened her grip on the figure, searching for things to say. "It's rough in places and ... smooth in places, too."

"Anything else?" Corrie asked.

"It's cold ... like stone."

"Yes, cold," said Corrie, as if Kat had at last solved a very simple riddle. "Now make a wish," he said.

"What?" Kat opened her eyes again.

"Hold the figure tight in your hand and make a wish," said Corrie.

"Is this some kind of joke?" said Kat trying to pass the figure back to him.

"Please," he said, refusing to take it.

"A wish?" she said, mockingly.

"A wish," he insisted.

Kat closed her eyes, thought for a moment, before making a secret wish. When she opened her eyes again Corrie was looking at her, closely, trying to gauge her reaction.

"Now what?" she said.

"Did you wish?" said Corrie.

"Yes."

"Did you feel anything?"

"What?"

"Did anything change? Was anything different?"

"It might help if I knew what you were expecting," she said.

Corrie took the figure back. It felt warm ... not warm like before, a more dilute warmth. The transferred heat of Kat's hand, nothing more.

"It has power," said Corrie.

"Power to grant wishes?" said Kat, unable to conceal the scorn in her voice.

"Power to grant wishes ... sort of," said Corrie. He told Kat about the morning bike ride and how by wishing he had managed to cut short his trip. But even as he was telling the story it didn't sound very convincing.

"And you think that was the bishop or whatever it is?" said Kat.

"It happened with Sal," said Corrie, "just now."

"Sal?" said Kat.

"I was coming to see you and when I opened the gate Sal rushed at me. I closed my eyes and wished that Sal wouldn't bite me. When I opened them again Sal was tied up and couldn't reach me," said Corrie.

"The dog's been tied up ever since my great-aunt died. Nothing magical about that," said Kat.

"But the figure grew warm each time," said Corrie.

"From your own fingers I shouldn't wonder," said Kat

Her explanations sounded more reasonable than his. Even Corrie could see that. But then she hadn't heard the voice or felt the figure grow warm and then cold again at the granting of each of Corrie's wishes.

"It was the figure," said Corrie. "I know it was."

Kat laughed. "Well, it didn't grant any wishes of mine," she said pointing at the sky.

Corrie looked up at the clouds churning grey

and swollen above them.

"I wished for glorious sunshine for the rest of the holiday," said Kat.

"What about the frost?" said Corrie suddenly remembering the web of silver tracery that had covered his window that first morning.

"What frost?"

"Your mum knows something about it too," said Corrie also remembering what Kat's mother had said to him.

"You spoke with her?"

"I was looking for you," said Corrie. "She knows."

"About the frost?" said Kat.

"About the warning," said Corrie. "She said it too."

"You mustn't pay heed to anything she says. She makes things up all the time. I told you. She's always telling stories. What did she say?" said Kat.

"She said 'She will come,'" said Corrie.

"What?"

"She said 'She will come.'"

"You don't think she maybe meant me?" said Kat, arching her eyebrow once again.

Corrie had to agree that that was a more reasonable explanation.

"Look," said Kat, "it could be a chess piece … a mitre-less bishop, perhaps. Or it could be just a figure. If not Noah, then a saint or something. St Francis! He had something to do with birds, didn't he?"

Corrie had to admit that from where Kat was

standing St Francis made more sense. It was a less interesting theory than the one Corrie wanted; less exciting and less mysterious. Perhaps he wanted the less ordinary explanation too much, so much that it made him see links where none existed and made him dream of voices and magic. Corrie began to doubt himself.

"St Francis?" he asked.

Kat was already walking away from him. "Why not?" she said.

He could not think of a reason why not.

"What will you do with it?"

Corrie wrapped it back in the handkerchief and hurried after her.

"What will you do with it?" she asked again.

"I don't know," he said.

"Might be worth something, you know," said Kat.

"I have to keep it," said Corrie.

"Have to?" said Kat.

He didn't know why he had said "have to." He must have meant "want to." He did want to keep it.

"I want to keep it," he said, correcting himself for her benefit.

"It's up to you," she said.

They walked along the beach leaving the tail of cottages further behind. The high tide line was still littered with the sea's flotsam and jetsam washed up on the back of the earlier storm.

"How was your bike ride then?" said Kat, turning away from a dead bird.

"About the same as last year ... and the year

before that," said Corrie. "It's the same every year."

"So do you do a lot of cycling then?"

Corrie shook his head and laughed. "Once a year ... usually in the first week of the holiday. Then never again until the following summer."

They both laughed.

Corrie lifted up the pink undressed body of a doll from the sand. The head was missing and so was one arm. Water and sand spilled from the empty arm socket. They laughed again.

"I bet there's a story behind this," said Corrie.

"Baby doll lost-at-sea nightmare," said Kat adopting an American accent and a dramatic pose.

"One-armed attempt to swim the Atlantic ends in tragedy," said Corrie sweeping his hand through the air as if outlining a sensational news headline.

Corrie tossed the doll down towards the water.

"Oh, don't you *have* to keep it?" mocked Kat. "Don't you *want* to keep it? Maybe this is who the voice was talking about when it said 'she will come.'"

Corrie did not laugh so heartily at this joke. Still clutching "St Francis" he put his hand into his jacket pocket. His knuckles brushed against the hard cover of the book he'd forgotten to show her.

"It's just a joke," said Kat.

"Do you read Gaelic?" he asked.

"What?" said Kat.

"Can you read Gaelic?" he asked again.

"Is this another one of your games?" she said.

"Another riddle to solve?"

He pulled the book out from his pocket. Some of the pages had worked their way free of the covers. Corrie tried to push them back together.

"I found this book," he said, "... in the cottage."

"And this one just leapt off the shelf and into your hand?" said Kat.

It hadn't leapt into his hand, but it had come to him. That's what Corrie thought. But he didn't think it would help to tell Kat that.

"Not exactly," said Corrie. "Here, look ... Can you read it or not?"

Kat took one of the loose pages and scanned the lines of text, working her way quickly down to the bottom of the page.

"Well?" said Corrie.

"I can read a bit," said Kat. "Not very well ... but a bit."

"And?" said Corrie.

Kat took another page and poured over the words.

"What's it about?" he said.

She took another page.

"Kat?" said Corrie.

"The pages are all mixed up," she said.

"Just the first bit. The first few pages just fell out," he explained.

"Are there pictures in the book?" asked Kat, taking some more pages.

"No ... No pictures. Just words," said Corrie, offering her the whole thing.

"Then how did you know?" said Kat.

"Know what? What's it about? Come on … tell me. Tell me," he insisted.

"It's my mother's story," said Kat.

"What story?" said Corrie.

"The one I told you. The sea dragon and the fisherman. It's the same story. How did you know if you don't know Gaelic?"

"I didn't," said Corrie.

"There has to be a reasonable explanation," said Kat leafing through the rest of the book.

"There doesn't," said Corrie excitedly. He drew the carved walrus-tusk figure from his pocket again. "I told you, Kat. It has power."

"No," she said, still turning the pages.

"It's *not* St Francis," said Corrie.

Kat did not reply.

"It's not St Francis. It's not Noah. And it's not a bishop," he said.

Still she did not look up from the pages of the book.

"It's the magician from the story. It's the wise man who beat the sea dragon back into the sea with his staff. I know it is."

"It's just one of my mother's stories!" said Kat.

She stopped turning the pages, fixing Corrie with her gaze. He felt like she was trying to see through him.

"What?" he said.

"Tell me this is some kind of joke, Corrie."

"No, it's not," he said. "It doesn't make sense. I can't explain it either."

She turned the book round so that Corrie could see the final page. At the top in bold print was the title and underneath a short paragraph that ended half way down the page.

"Read it," said Kat.

"What?" said Corrie.

"The title," said Kat.

Corrie was puzzled "It's in Gaelic."

She was still staring through him.

"*Gaoth*. That's the only Gaelic word I know. And I only learned that the other day. From you. What does it say?" Corrie asked helplessly.

"*Thig I.*"

"I don't understand. What is it?"

"What you said," she replied, her voice almost a whisper.

"What?" he said.

"What you said before."

"What d'you mean?" said Corrie.

"She will come," said Kat.

"She will come?" echoed Corrie.

Kat turned back to face him. "That's what it says ... *Thig I*. She will come."

7. She Will Come

"So what else does it say?" said Corrie.

She was looking towards the cottages, her back half turned to him. Her hair had blown across her cheek, like a ragged scarf, so that Corrie couldn't see the expression on her face.

"Does it say who *she* is and *when* she will come? Read the last page." Corrie, reached for the remains of the book still in her hands.

"I think we should tell someone about this," said Kat, ignoring his questions.

Corrie looked down at the sand. He hadn't been sure of telling Kat about the chess piece's powers and her scepticism had been entirely expected. If the book had been nothing more than an old book, Corrie would have been satisfied that his imagination was working overtime in search of something, some excitement, to escape the boredom of another summer holiday in Uig. But it was all slotting together like a jigsaw and if the picture still remained fuzzy and difficult to see then that was because they had some pieces of the puzzle left to find.

"Tell someone what?" said Corrie.

"I don't know ... anything." Kat, turned now to face him.

Corrie could see that she was frightened. He hadn't reckoned on this.

"What does it say?" said Corrie, holding up the last page, which had also split away from the cover.

Kat took the age-yellowed paper and began reading.

Corrie waited impatiently, listening to the spit and gutteral murmur of Kat trying to decipher the words on the page.

"It says she will come again bringing winter in her rings once more ... or something like that ... bringing winter even into summer. I can't quite make sense of it. It says she will come on the back of storms and grey seas." Her finger danced around on the page, underlining over and over the words that she was finding difficult to translate.

"There's so much here that I can't make out. It says she will come when the old one steps up out of the sand. Then something about the stick that doesn't bend and feathers that burn."

Corrie could see Kat's finger running again and again under the last two lines on the page, searching for the meaning of words.

"What else?" Corrie interrupted.

"I don't know," said Kat. "There's something about the story having a different voice or a different storyteller. I'm not sure. It's very confusing. I can't make out the rest."

Kat gave up and let her hand drop to her side.

The sullen grey clouds seemed to hang lower in the sky than was possible, like a great dark weight waiting to fall down on the people of Uig.

"*She* must be the sea dragon," said Kat.

"Yes," said Corrie. "That would fit."

"We must tell someone," Kat said again.

Corrie shook his head.

"If my aunt was still alive, we could have told her," said Kat. "She knew things. That's what my mother says. She understood things that others didn't. She'd have been able to explain this. Maybe we could tell my mother. Maybe she could help."

"No," said Corrie.

"But the sea dragon ..." said Kat, her eyes half shut against the hiss and spit of the rain that had just started.

"It's just a story." He grabbed at the page in Kat's hand and stuffed it with the rest of the book into his coat pocket. "That's what they'll say: it's just a story."

The chill of the rain was surprising. The wind set up a howling moan that seemed to move around them like a circling beast. Corrie took Kat's arm and pulled her up the beach and into the dunes. They crouched down behind a bank of sand patched over with spiky marram grass.

"It says she will come on the back of storms and grey seas, bringing winter with her," said Kat, her voice a loud call lifting upwards and carried away on the wind.

"You've holidayed enough in Uig to know that

storms and cold winds are not unusual in the summer," said Corrie, huddling close to her.

She was shivering, a jerky shaking that began at her shoulders and spread through her. "See," she said, through gritted teeth. "This is isn't exactly normal weather ... even for here!"

She pointed. There, on the sleeve of her coat, was a dissolving ice crystal.

"Snow!"

"Hail," Corrie corrected her. "It's just a story. You said so yourself."

She tried to speak again, but her teeth clicked together uncontrollably.

"We'd best get you home," said Corrie, beginning to shiver himself. He stood up, his head rising above the crest of the dune and catching the icy blast driving off the sea. He tried pulling Kat to her feet, but she was heavy and unwilling.

Corrie ducked back down.

"You'll have to help me," he said urgently.

Kat trembled with the cold, shuddering like someone in a fit.

"We can't stay here. It's too cold," said Corrie.

She looked up at him.

"We've had snow in June before," said Corrie. "It's just a story."

She shook her head.

"Come on ... get up," he said, tugging at her elbow.

The lids of her eyes, blue and shiny from the chill rain, drooped heavily.

"Come on!" Corrie yelled, still pulling at her arm. But he too felt his strength leaving him. He fell to his knees in the sand. "You have to help," he shouted.

The wind had changed direction so that the bank of sand no longer offered any protection. The cold came at them again, wet and icy; the wind too, churning up the sand and flinging it at them in stinging bursts. The howling of the wind had also changed; rising now to a fearful scream that hurt their ears.

"No!" he shouted, but Corrie couldn't hear his own cry above the storm.

Then he remembered the chess piece. He fumbled in his pocket. His fingers, numb with cold, fished clumsily about for the ivory figure. He found one corner of the handkerchief and pulled it out. Some of the loose pages of the book spilled free and were whisked away on the wind. The chess piece rolled out onto the sand.

Corrie scrabbled after it, and as soon as his fingers closed round the piece of bone he felt it … a sudden warmth: a warmth that he had felt in his bedroom when he had first picked up the figure; a warmth that entered through his fingers and spread through his very being. A life-giving warmth. He felt a strengthening of his own will, a hardening of his determination.

"No!" he cried again … and this time he heard it.

He turned to Kat and curled her unresponsive fingers round the chess piece. Then his hand closed around hers. He wished that Kat could share the warmth too and almost before the wish was made Corrie could feel the cold disappearing from her.

The wind continued to drive the ice and sand at

them, changing the whole map of the dunes with the force of each sweeping attack. Corrie leaned over Kat, sheltering her from the battering blast.

"It's real," breathed Kat. She was no longer shivering and the colour was returning to her skin. "It's real," she repeated, her fingers still clasped round the piece of carved ivory.

Corrie did not know if she meant the magic of the chess piece or the story of the sea dragon. Both seemed to him to be part of the same dream from which he might wake at any moment.

"We can't stay here," he said.

A clink of metal against metal sounded. *This could all be a dream,* Corrie thought. It sounded again ... and again. Corrie was reminded of glass rattling in the window of his holiday bedroom. Corrie knew that's how dreams worked sometimes: a noise made in the real world was heard in the dream world where it was changed into something fantastic.

"Look," said Kat, pointing over Corrie's shoulder.

He turned, looking to where she pointed.

"It's a door."

The wind had uncovered a series of rough planks fastened together with metal bolts. It was still half hidden under the sand, but a loop of metal lifted and fell in the wind making the clinking noise that had attracted their attention.

They got up and ran the few yards to the wooden door. As if it really were a beast hounding them, the wind changed direction again, swirling around them, sending sheets of sand and sleet at their backs.

Corrie seized hold of the metal ring. It was heavy and ridged. Had he looked more closely, he would have seen a braided ring with a dragon's head swallowing its own tail in an unbroken iron circle. But Corrie was more intent on getting the door open. He wrenched at the handle, hearing the wood complain ... but it did not give.

"Help me dig it out," said Corrie, already shovelling the sand away with both hands.

Kat, who was still clutching the chess piece, pressed it into the pocket of her jacket and fell to the task of uncovering the door.

It was bigger than they had at first thought, with three large hinges on its left-hand side, and arched at the top where some of the wood had split and splintered at the edges, leaving sharp jagged cracks through which sand disappeared, but through which it was impossible to see.

They had expected to be fighting against the wind but strangely it seemed to be assisting them. The wet sleet slackened and the screaming dropped to a hushed whisper, like the murmur of excitement that settles on a crowd and signals the anticipation of something long awaited.

"Can't see anything," said Corrie, perched half way up the slope of sand with one eye pressed up against the widest fissure. "It's too dark."

Then the door was uncovered.

Close to them the wind seemed to drop, as though holding its breath for fear that the slightest movement at that moment might interfere with events. Only feet beyond them the air still moved, and sand and sleet danced a mad dance.

It was as though they were in a bubble of calm. A cold bubble nevertheless.

Corrie yanked at the door again. It lifted with a groan, then settled back with a thump that echoed deep within. Kat put her hands beside Corrie's and together they pulled.

When it was a quarter of the way open Corrie slipped both hands underneath the door so that he could get a better purchase. The door lifted more easily then, though one of the hinges twisted and snapped and left the door hanging askew. Kat leaned against the open door, half lying on it, whilst Corrie fetched several rocks to wedge it open.

All the while the wind barely breathed, moved further off and the sleet, falling now in an airy drizzle, settled on them like tiny spots of light, melting into shiny glass jewels or sequins. It remained cold, but charged with the warmth given to them by the carved magician, and working so busily at unearthing the door, neither noticed.

The threshold was concealed under several feet of sand that had leaked through the cracks in the door, but beyond they could see stairs plunging downwards into darkness. Corrie climbed over the sand and stood on the first step looking at the steep descent into blackness. He had to crouch, for although the door was taller than him, the stair passageway was not. Cut into rock, the tunnel walls were rough and sharp, but the stairs were round-edged as though centuries of passing feet had worn them away.

"Wait!" Kat ordered, as Corrie put his foot onto the second step. "The wind's stopped."

Corrie looked up at her.

"The sleet and the rain too," said Kat.

Corrie glanced at grey clouds still churning threateningly above them. "So?"

"It's passed. We don't need to go down."

"We do," said Corrie.

"No!"

"Don't you see?" he said.

"No, I don't see. See what?" she stared back at him angrily.

"We've been brought here. Something has led us to this door. We have to go on. It's the next step. It will make sense, I know it will. We have to go down. We just have to."

"I don't understand," said Kat.

Corrie searched for something to say to her; a way to convince her. Why he was so certain, he could not say. The uneven steps beckoned to him, from where the light stopped and darkness began.

"We have to go," he muttered, half to himself.

"Can you smell it?" Kat nodded towards the blackness.

Corrie sniffed the air.

"It's like before," she said, "... like the hole on the beach, when we met ... it's like rotting vegetables."

It *was* the same fetid smell he had uncovered on pulling the wooden fence post out of the sand; the stale smell of decay. This time Corrie recognised the smell and remembered. It was not like rotten vegetables, no ... more like the smell of death. The summer Corrie and his father had crouched in ditches, watching lapwings bobbing and bowing in the heather, they had stumbled upon the matted remains of a dead sheep, half submerged in foul-smelling ditchwater. Crows had ripped open its stomach and picked out a gaping hole through which Corrie could see a mess of decaying innards and its exposed ribs. The sheep had been dead some time, but the head had still been recognisable from the curling yellow horns and the bared grin of its crooked teeth. The eyes had gone and Corrie remembered looking into the dark and empty sockets, looking for the point where life ended and death began. There was nothing to see in those blind holes, but Corrie had bent closer ... until he smelled it. And here was the same thing ... the same rank odour of death and decay.

"We have to go down," said Corrie again, this time to her. "I just know we do!"

"I don't understand," said Kat again.

"Me neither," he responded vaguely.

"Then why?" said Kat.

Corrie really didn't know why. It would have been easier not to go down: easier to walk back along the beach to the cottages; easier to just walk away from this ... from the book and the ivory chess piece; easier to let the chessman gather dust on some high mantelpiece, its story unexplored. It would have been simpler to close the wooden door in the sand. It would have been quite straightforward ... and so much safer, too.

But Corrie couldn't do that. He felt somehow chosen, though not in any way that made sense. He knew with inexplicable certainty, that this was another part of the whole puzzle. The chess-piece figure, the book with the invisible braided ring on its first page, the story of the sea dragon, the ice in the summer rain, the door in the sand — he knew they were all connected in an important way, but he didn't know how. Without going down he would never know; the jigsaw would never be complete.

"It's all connected," said Corrie.

"Yes," said Kat. "That's what frightens me."

"Where's the chess piece?" said Corrie.

"What?" said Kat.

"The chess piece ... put it in your hand and hold tight," said Corrie.

He didn't know what prompted him to this. It was as though a voice inside his own head was telling him what to say, a voice that he recognised. The same voice he heard in the dark of his bedroom in the cottage. Quieter this time, perhaps. More in his head than before. But the voice the same.

Kat put her hand in her pocket and brought out the figure. It stared up at her from the palm of her hand. She could already feel its warmth.

"Hold it tight," he repeated. He wasn't sure why he was telling her this. Somehow it seemed to make sense. That's all he knew.

Kat gripped it so hard that it dug into the soft palm of her hand.

"Now close your eyes," said Corrie.

Kat closed her eyes, still gripping the walrus-tusk carving.

All at once the wind was back again, pushing her towards the hole in the ground. She couldn't make sense of it. On the one hand, the storm was real. She could feel that. The buffeting wind and the driving sleet were real. But somehow, even to Kat, it also felt like it belonged to the story of the sea dragon, and to the little chess-piece figure she held. It was like the wind was being used to drive her down into the hole. She didn't understand why. The full force of the storm returned; great heavy gobs of sea spit soaked her back. The sand whipped at her legs. It was as if she and Corrie were being herded, like sheep; like she'd seen Sal do with the loose sheep on the hills.

She gripped the magician tighter, till she thought it would hurt … but it never did. She was warm again, and though the elements still blasted at her back, Kat could no longer feel them. Then she saw her. A woman, as if in a dream, kneeling on snow. A young woman, her face half masked under a black shawl pulled down low over her head. The woman looked up at Kat. Her blue lips were moving, calling, but no words came.

Corrie saw Kat drop to her knees, the chess piece held in front of her, her eyes closed.

"Come on," he shouted from the entrance to the tunnel.

Kat strained to hear what the woman was shouting. The woman's cold clouded breath carried her prayers upwards, but no sound cut through the silence that lay between them. The woman raised her hands, beseechingly. The shawl slipped back from her face, revealing her eyes spilling tears; tears that froze to ice on her pale cheeks. Kat recognised those eyes, recognised something in them, though she had never seen them before. Something glinted in the open palm of the woman's hand. Kat looked, then dropped the bone figure in fright. The vision of the kneeling woman thinned to nothing in an instant.

"How can it be?" she whispered.

Corrie did not hear her. He snatched the chess piece out of the sand and pulled Kat to her feet. "Come on," he yelled again.

"Did you see her?"

"Who?" yelled Corrie.

"A woman … kneeling in the snow. In her hand she had something I've seen before. It's part of this. Don't ask me how. It just is." She looked to Corrie. "It doesn't make sense. I thought it was just a story. I thought it was just something my mother told me. And her mother told her. A story from a book. The one you showed me. But it's more than that."

"We have to go," he said.

Kat shook her head. "I can't," she said, "I can't." She didn't understand why she couldn't go, any more than Corrie understood why he had to. She shook her head and pulled away. "I can't," she repeated and she turned from him and ran back to the beach.

The wind opened up a path for her and closed again behind her. Corrie watched her go.

8. The Hall of Forgotten Battles

Corrie watched until he could no longer make out the red blur of Kat's jacket flapping away from him. His cheeks burned and his eyes stung. He had to rub away the salt tears so that he could stay focused on her. Even when he could no longer pick Kat out, Corrie remained at the top of the steps looking back at the grey gloom that hung over Uig.

"She will come," said a voice. It was the same voice as before. Corrie looked down at the figure in his hand with its bulging frightened eyes. "She will come," said the voice again. It was a flat voice, a matter-of-fact voice, delivered without any emotion. Corrie could not tell if the voice was a thought inside his own head or something spoken by the chess piece in his hand.

"Who?" he asked, unable to decide any more who the "she" referred to. He hoped it referred to Kat. "Who will come?" he repeated. There was no reply. Corrie kicked his frustration against the buckled door hinge. Then he turned his back on the light and began to descend the stone steps.

The ceiling and walls of the tunnel were damp, running here and there with a silky green sweat that dripped and trailed onto the steps below. Corrie had to move slowly and deliberately so as not to lose his footing. At first, the grey light from the door was bright enough to guide his way, but each step took him deeper into blackness. When he stopped to look back he was surprised to see how small the rectangle of light had grown, and how far above him it was.

It was cold in the tunnel. The air was chill and damp. He thought of stopping and retracing his steps but his shirt, stuck to his back, was like a cold hand pressing him onwards.

Corrie held the figure of the magician up before him. Gripping it tightly, he made a wish. It began to glow, like a dim torch in the night-black darkness. which grew slowly brighter and warmer, sending a white light ahead of him. Warmth spread through him, just as he had felt before, until the cold and the damp were again as nothing to him.

Corrie edged his way further down. He could see his own breath thicken into clouds of mist that drifted away from him, thinning and vanishing before him. His fingers brushed against ice on the walls and the brittle pools on the steps cracked and crunched under his feet. Still the steps led down into a frozen darkness.

When the steps ran out, Corrie again looked back. He could not see the door now, nor the ghost of its feeble light. Even a tiny pinprick of light, no bolder than the smallest star, would have offered some comfort. Corrie lifted the light in front again. The steps had stopped at the entrance to a small chamber, no bigger, it seemed, than Corrie's bedroom in the cottage.

"Is this it?" he wondered. His voice echoed off the walls; back and forth, multiplying into a grumbling crowd of voices murmuring complaint. He lifted the chess-piece magician higher and swung his arm in a slow arc through the air. The light washed over the walls making the shadows jump away from him.

"I've come down here for this?" said Corrie, swinging his arm through the air a second time. Only the stone replied, sending back a dull senseless echo of his broken words.

At the end of his third sweep the light fell on a low jagged arch almost completely hidden in a dip in the wall. The chess piece seemed to lead him to it and Corrie crossed the cave to stand before the small opening. It was placed so that he had to bend awkwardly to see into it and, even then, waving the light in at the entrance revealed very little. What he could see beyond the arch was a low ceilinged passageway that sloped gently downwards and curled out of sight to the right. It was wide enough even for a large man to crawl through on his hands and knees. Corrie shivered. He remembered having seen a programme once about potholers exploring deep underground. It had been somewhere in Wales. He had watched with anxious fascination as they'd teased their bodies between the narrowest of cracks and threaded through impossibly tight crevices. Corrie had felt light-headed and nauseous just watching.

"This is the way," said the voice of the chess piece. Like before, the voice was inside Corrie's head but at the same time seemed to come from the figure in his hand. There was no echo to the words, so that Corrie wondered at this feeling that the chess piece was talking to him. He held onto the figure, tight in his grasp, and moved through the arch into the passageway ahead of him. Crouched down and with his head bent, Corrie was able to shuffle crab-like along the floor without dropping to his knees. The passageway twisted and turned like the regular slithering of a giant worm or snake burrowing down to the very centre of the world.

The way forward was suddenly blocked by a door; like the door on the beach, although perhaps twice the size, and made of the same heavy wood with the same metal studs. This time Corrie noticed the handle: the unbroken ring of plaited metal; the dragon's open mouth with its tail between its teeth. The shock of recognition was like a sharp smack across his face, knocking him off balance. Corrie stumbled, falling heavily against the wooden door. It gave under his weight and swung inwards with a scream of rusted metal. The chess-piece figure dropped from his hand. Corrie heard it clatter across the floor, though he could not see it in the abrupt darkness that wrapped itself around him. He felt immediately cold. Panic awoke and rose up from the corner where it had slept, rose up to its full height and roared. The air shook and Corrie's frightened cry beat nightmare wings about his head, again and again.

The minutes ran one into another, rushing to keep pace with the drumming of Corrie's heart. He waited for his eyes to adjust to the darkness, as they always did when his mother switched off the bedroom light at home. But this was a very different kind of darkness. Perhaps he *was* just dreaming. At any moment he would wake and find himself in his cottage bedroom with the shutters closed. The minutes piled one on top of the other and he did not wake. Corrie felt them pressing down on him like a great weight. He began to shiver, his teeth to chatter and his body to shake.

"M-m-must find him." Corrie crawled slowly across the floor. His hands fluttered blindly in front of him. When his fingers settled on the chess piece it was as if they had found each other. The ivory was still warm. Corrie clutched it to him and mouthed some kind of a prayer.

It was several minutes before Corrie opened his eyes again, but when he did he found himself kneeling in an enormous cavern; vaulted like a cathedral with magnificent carved pillars of rock rising like giant trees up to the ceiling where they branched out in broad fans that supported the rock. The floor was smooth and flat, covered with a chess board arrangement of red and cream tiles. The walls were hung with huge tapestries stiffened by frost and fringed with gold and silver cord.

"What is this place?" Corrie whispered.

"This is the Hall of Forgotten Battles," said the voice of the magician. This time Corrie was certain that the voice he heard was coming from the figure of the chess piece.

Corrie got to his feet. "Forgotten Battles?" he said, his voice sounding thin and insubstantial in that great hall.

Corrie felt the figure, small in his hand, pulling him forward, leading him further into the chamber. The magician led him to the first tapestry and Corrie lifted up the light so that he could see. It was a fine piece of work woven in threads of yellows and reds, greens and blacks, as vibrantly coloured as the day it had been cut from the loom. In the centre a warrior held high the black severed head of a bear.

"This is Jarl Silverhair and Gnud," said the magician. "Gnud was a bear that stood taller than twenty men, so tall it is said that it blocked out the sun and its shadow stretched across oceans. When it moved the mountains of the earth trembled and everywhere the ground cracked and split. Such a bear was never seen before nor since. Gnud's claws were sharper than the sharpest swords and it could cut down whole forests with a single swipe. Whole villages disappeared to feed its vast appetite. Jarl Silverhair it was who one day killed that bear. Afterwards there were songs that told of his great deeds and his great unhappiness."

The magician led Corrie on to the next hanging tapestry without explaining how Jarl Silverhair had managed to defeat the great bear, Gnud.

"Siggeir the Quick could run faster than the sun, so fast that he could outrun the night." The tapestry showed a fair-haired warrior with a broken sword and spear standing on top of a hill of black-bearded corpses.

They moved onto the next without stopping.

"Egil War-dancer," said the magician. "At only twelve years old he had the strength of ten bulls and played his sword like a song."

The line of tapestries stretched almost from one end of the great hall to the other.

"Stump-Snidil and Hild. Snidil had only one leg, the other was bitten off by a tusked boar and replaced by a stump of wood. Though he was as sure footed as any goat, he was ever after known as Stump-Snidil. It was his wife, Hild, who wove these tapestries. She was as deft with the halberd as she was with the shuttle, for she was trained in the skills of knighthood even though she was a queen."

They did not stop at every tapestry. Some the magician passed by without comment, some he referred to with a single name sung out loud as though greeting a long lost friend.

"Rognvald the Toothless ... I have seen this man catch spears in flight and hurl them back with the force of thunderbolts."

Rognvald stared out from the canvas with a gap-toothed grin stitched across his face. He held a spear in each hand and at his feet lay the bodies of warriors he had slain.

They moved on.

"Bent-Busla ... a woman highly skilled in magic who always provided favourable winds for the ships."

They stopped before one canvas that was twice as long as the rest and without understanding why Corrie bowed his head. It was as if the magician and not just his voice was inside Corrie.

"The Battle of the Kings," said the magician solemnly. "Sometimes called the Battle of Gorfin, for it was fought in the valley of that name. Thorvald, Borgar, Glammad and Gorm all fell in this fray. And many more kings besides."

Corrie counted fifteen stitched golden crowns lined up across the top of the tapestry.

When they arrived at the penultimate tapestry in the line they halted again.

"The First of the Battles of Shrak," announced the magician.

His voice lowered and Corrie's hand shook.

"And beyond, the Second Battle, when Shrak returned in the undoing of things," said the magician. Corrie knew that he meant the last tapestry in the hall, but all their attention was still on the first battle.

"This great battle, the first against the worm called Shrak, is remembered more than the rest we have passed, but remembered only by a small number in your world. You have heard it told. She told it to you."

"I don't know of any Shrak," said Corrie.

"Shrak, the hoary worm — sometimes called the serpent or dragon of the sea. Thrice round this island she did wrap her icy form and summer was made into winter. You have heard the tale."

"The story of the sea dragon. Yes ... Kat told me. But she couldn't tell me why? Why did the dragon come here?"

"I wish I could tell you that it was sent as a curse against the people of the island, a punishment for some unforgivable misdeed wrought by the islanders against a great king who sailed the seas in a long ship decorated with silver and gold, its sails dipped in blood. Or a magician spurned by the woman he loved might have brought down the wrath of the worm on the island. Something like that would make sense and I wish that it was so. But this is not the truth. There is evil in the world," said the voice, "plain and simple. Who knows where it comes from? Not the very wise, nor the very old. Good will always stand against evil. That is written in the stories of all our fathers, and the stories of our fathers' fathers. Shrak is no different."

Corrie's attention returned to the tapestry before him. He examined this tapestry more closely than all the rest that they had passed. It showed a dark grey rock with a green dragon coiled three times round its base. Its claws were sunk into the stone and a white mist curled from its mouth. Level with the head of the dragon, on a frozen sea was a ship with torn sails. Corrie could just make out two figures in the prow of the ship; one kneeling in prayer, the other stirring the sea with the point of a long staff. Where the staff touched the water a small red flame danced and above the two figures circled a tiny silver bird.

"Is that you in the ship?" asked Corrie.

"It was so long ago that even to me it seems as if it were someone else," replied the magician.

"Then it was *you* who defeated the dragon."

"It was Corvald the Rower who brought me to the dragon but I could not have defeated it alone," said the magician.

"Corvald the Rower," Corrie repeated. *His name and Corvald's so close. Too close,* he thought, *for this to be an accident.*

"It was Corvald who brought the pieces together," said the magician. "That was his role."

Corrie looked again. It was not really to scale. The rock was more than a rock; it had to be the island. His eyes settled on a small lone figure kneeling in the middle of the island; a woman. Corrie knew this though there was no way of telling from the tiny stitches that picked out the figure. A long black shawl fell like water about her shoulders and she held her cupped hands up in the air. The figure was too small to see what it was she held, but a single stitch of gold thread glinted in the centre of her raised hands.

"Katyen," said the magician.

"I don't understand," said Corrie.

"That is how a battle begins to be forgotten … an important detail is left out in the retelling, then another piece is lost in someone's memory. Soon the story makes no sense and in time it is told no more, is forgotten. Katyen of the Ring … she has been left out."

"Katyen of the Ring?" said Corrie.

"You have seen the ring, too, I think."

Corrie thought he knew without asking what ring the Magician meant. It was everywhere; a raised emblem on the box that he had found on the beach; embossed on the flyleaf of the book with the Gaelic retelling of the sea dragon story; and carved round the hem of the chess-piece magician's robe. It was also on the door handle to the Hall of Forgotten Battles.

"It is a magic ring and its magic is older and more powerful than any I can summon; strong enough to keep Shrak in thrall for all eternity. Only she has broken free again as she did once before." Here the magician seemed to draw Corrie's attention to the last tapestry. Beside it Corrie could see that there was room for one more.

"The Second Battle," said the magician. "The ring was broken then, too. Just as now. And like knot-work when its single thread is broken, the pattern is unravelling. The ring has not been handed on. It has been dropped in the space between the living and the dead. That is enough, and the unending thread has been broken; the magic broken too. It is all in the weaving of the ring. We must weave it whole again."

Corrie was distracted, not looking at what was in front of him, but staring off into the dark space on the wall left for a final tapestry.

"We knew this day would come and that is why we have waited here. We knew there would be one more battle, the third and last of the battles with Shrak. That is why we have left one space on the wall; space for one more working of cloth and thread. This is what we have waited for. The ring must be remade one last time … or stay broken forever. That is why she will come."

"Who's been waiting? You said 'we.'"

Without answering and without explaining what was there on the last completed tapestry, the Second Battle tapestry, the chess-piece magician, still clasped in Corrie's hand, seemed to lead Corrie away. They passed the blank space on the wall of tapestries and Corrie wondered what it would show when all this was over ... what was meant by the final battle that the magician spoke of?

Weaving between the lines of pillars, the magician led the boy into the centre of the hall. It was like standing in the middle of an enormous forest clearing, with pillars like great trees on either side. At the far end of the hall a flight of steps had been cut into the rock and they swept up to a high open portal, the gaping entrance to another chamber.

Two carved figures, grim-faced giant warriors with swords and shields and twin-bladed battle-axes, flanked the doorway. They stared wide-eyed and crazed over Corrie's head.

"Where does that go?" Corrie demanded.

"That is the House of the Guardians," said the magician.

They climbed the steps until they stood on the threshold of this inner room. Corrie held the chess piece before him so that the House of the Guardians was lit with the magician's bright white light. Corrie was amazed at what he saw. The walls were lined from floor to high ceiling with shelves cut into the rock, and each shelf was filled with line upon line of carved chess-piece figures; whole armies of them. Some had been disturbed and had toppled from their shelves. There were carved ivory figures lying like casualties of war on the floor of the chamber. Corrie bent to inspect the pieces.

They were just like the figures he had seen in the museum exhibition he had visited twice with his parents: helmeted knights on horseback with tilted lances; mitred bishops, all armed with curling croziers and some clutching books; seated kings with swords across their laps and queens with worried faces and hands raised to their cheeks in alarm; and warriors with their swords drawn and their sheilds up. Some of the warriors gnashed their teeth against the tops of their shields and Corrie recalled that these were the mad Bezerkers. The figures ranged on one side of the room were a rusty red colour, a kind of dried blood-red. The figures on the other side were plain ivory. But red or plain Corrie recognised them as the Lewis chessmen, except that there were so many more ... hundreds of them ... thousands.

"The Guardians?" said Corrie sceptically.

"These are the Guardians," affirmed the magician.

There was so much that Corrie still did not understand and so much that he couldn't altogether believe. It all seemed so unreal as if he was dreaming, though where exactly the dream began Corrie couldn't decide. Sea dragons and chess-piece armies, underground halls and magic knot-work rings ... they all belonged to a different Uig from the dull holidays he was used to. Corrie wasn't even sure that he didn't prefer the long days with nothing to do and no one to do it with. He was scared, in the way you can be in dreams without really knowing what it is that you are scared of.

"Why am I here?" said Corrie.

"I have told you. The ring has been broken," said the magician.

"I still don't understand."

"The ring must be forged again … forged in battle one last time. At the very first, I stood with Corvald the Rower and Katyen of the Ring; our power combined. So it shall be again. She will come."

"Who?"

"You will know when she is here," said the magician.

9. The Ring

A small knot of mourners, black-tied and sour-faced, had gathered in the sitting room of Kat's great-aunt's cottage. They were sipping strong sweet tea out of her great-aunt's best china, trying not to stare across at the mantelpiece clock. They looked up as one when she entered.

"Ah, Katrine."

Kat nodded to Murdo from the post office.

"It's a sad day for all of us, Katrine," he muttered, shaking his head and spilling tea into his saucer.

Kat nodded again and hurried away. At the open door of the dining-room she stopped. The curtains were drawn and on the table and below the window was her great-aunt's coffin with her great-aunt stretched out inside. The lid was in place. Just a wooden box to see. Kat had seen her great-aunt before the lid had been closed, briefly. *In death, at least, her great-aunt had lost some of the roughness from her features,* Kat thought. *She'd looked less in years, too.*

Kat turned from the door and rushed up the stairs.

"Is that you, Katrine?"

"Am I late?" said Kat, slipping out of her red jacket.

"I've laid out your black dress on your bed."

Kat's mother was sitting on one side of her great-aunt's bed, her arm hugging the shoulders of an elderly woman from the village. Kat couldn't see their faces.

"There's a black shawl, too. Hurry now."

Kat backed away from her great-aunt's room into her own. She shut the door behind her, then she sat on the edge of the bed next to the black dress and shawl. She held a piece of yellowed paper in her hand: soggy and torn … one of the spilled pages from Corrie's book. She had found it stuck to the gate, like a message delivered by the wind. At the top of the page was a name she did not recognise. It was not part of the story her mother had told to her and it unsettled her. Perhaps it was the similarity with her own name that surprised her, or maybe the feeling that there had always been something missing from the sea dragon tale, a feeling that she had always kept to herself. Maybe this was a missing piece. Kat read the name over and over as if trying to decipher some difficult code, as if searching between the words for something hidden.

"Katyen of the Ring. Katyen of the Ring. Katyen of the Ring."

She heard movement on the stairs. Her mother was helping the lady mourner back to the living room.

Kat ran her finger along the other lines of type, stumbling over some of the words as she struggled to translate.

"She saw the forest ... go away... disappear. To begin with just one tree at a time, but soon many of the trees together. The hills became bare and ... were never bare before and never less than bare thereafter. And the fires they fed could not be holding back the cold from the door, nor the cold from men's hearts. And Katyen of the Ring watched. And Katyen of the Ring wept. She wept and wept until her tears were all ... of them to ice. And she could not be crying again. The sea dragon made tighter its ... And Katyen of the Ring was on her knees. She was calling to the ghosts of the dead forest, the spirits that once dwelt there, and they did come to her when she bid them. And they danced in a circle around her. Round and round so fast that they did come together ... or join together. And then Corvald the fisherman brought the magician. And so Katyen had her magic Ring; something complete with the magician and Corvald, the fisherman, and Katyen. And the sea dragon would be sleeping inside that Ring and never waking until it be broken."

Kat had seen the woman kneeling in the snow: the shawl covering her head, her hands raised and a ring glinting in her open palm. Kat had recognised something in the woman's upturned eyes, something so close that each time she reached for it, it dissolved into mist. And the ring in her hand was one Kat had seen before ... so familiar to her that it could never be forgotten nor mistaken.

"Are you dressed yet, Katrine?" her mother called.

Kat hid the paper and began stripping off her wet jeans.

"Nearly," she replied.

She'd worn the black dress once before, to a party. It seemed odd to be wearing it to a funeral … her great-aunt's funeral. She tugged the stubborn zipper up to her neck, pulled the hem of the dress as low as it would go and drew a brush through her damp, tangled hair. Then she picked up the shawl.

"Katrine!"

Kat did not hear. She was running the shawl through her fingers, inspecting its black weave. It was a plain black and had been her great-aunt's. Kat held it to her face and breathed in. She could smell her great-aunt in the folds of black wool: the smell of her soap; her skin and hair; the smell of her rough hands. It was as if her great-aunt were still there, part of her caught in the weft and weave of the cloth. The kneeling woman had worn a black shawl too … just like the one Kat held in her hands. As the woman had raised her eyes to Kat's the shawl had slipped back to reveal a coiled plait of hair … red hair: red like her great-aunt's must have been when she was a young woman; red like her mother's; and like Kat's own hair now.

"Katyen of the Ring," Kat whispered, into the shawl. She sat back on the bed the pieces of the puzzle sliding slowly into place.

"Katrine! Everybody's waiting. Are you coming?"

"She will come!" said Kat.

Kat's mother swept into the room and began fussing over her daughter's hair and the neck of her dress. "They're all waiting downstairs. Are you alright? Is it the shawl? You can leave it if you like. It's not important."

"The ring, where's the ring?" Kat flicked the shawl over her head, wrapping it around her shoulders as she had seen her great-aunt do. "I need the ring."

"Everybody's waiting," her mother insisted.

"I need great-aunt's knot-work ring," repeated Kat.

Kat's mother sighed. "She said this would happen." She sat down on the bed beside Kat and reached one hand under her own shawl. "We should have come sooner, Kat. That's what your great-aunt Katherine wanted. She said so in her last letters. I thought there was time enough. She said she had things to tell you; important things she would not share with me. They were for you to hear and you only. She was anxious that we should get here before ..." She broke off from what she was saying.

"The ring?" prompted Kat, as gently as she could.

Kat's mother nodded. "She said you would need it soon; that I wouldn't understand, but that you would. Somehow you would. She was certain of that. It was the way of things." She brought out a sealed envelope with Katrine's name scrawled on the front in her great-aunt's spidery hand and held it out to her daughter.

Kat tore open the envelope. The ring fell out onto the bed. She knew it at once. It was the same. It was the same as she had seen before on her great-aunt's finger, the same as she had seen in the raised palm of the kneeling woman when she had knelt with Corrie's chess-piece magician in her hand.

A folded slip of paper fluttered like an injured bird to the floor. Kat's mother bent to pick it up, but Kat snatched it from her. It seemed to have been written in a gentler voice than she was used to from her great-aunt.

Dear Katrine,

the time has come sooner than I expected it would. My dear child, I had thought you would be here before now, before I passed over from this world into the next. You should have been here, with me, by my side. There is so much that has been kept from you, so much that I have not yet told you or have told you only in part, so much that I have kept to myself. Not even your mother has a share of what I must tell you now.

In truth, I had thought there would not be the need … but I see now that by waiting too long the chain has been broken, the chain that should have kept her bound. Perhaps that is as it was meant to be. Who can really know? The wheels turn with or without me. I think you will by now know of the foul worm of whom I speak.

This ring is yours now, Katrine, and you can no longer be a child. It passes to you, like it passed to me … the ring. Katyen's Ring. Like in the story … only this is something real. I have been its guardian; you will be more than this and I am sorry for it.

It is late. I cannot wait. You should be here. You should be here on the island. I fear the breaking of the ring. But broken or whole, it must pass to you. There can be no choice. Katyen is in you as she was in me. I can see that and you must feel it. You have to take the ring and its adventures, too, as I have done. The island depends on it. The island depends on you. And Shrak must sleep still and the ring be unbroken again. Only you can mend this. I think you will understand. I think you will know what to do.

from your Great-Aunt Katherine.

Kat picked up the Ring. It was a thin gold band, though it looked like three bands plaited together in an everlasting braid ... without beginning or end.

"Unbroken," whispered Kat. It was not what she had expected.

She had seen knot-work patterns before. They were everywhere: part of the culture; part of the landscape of the island; on everything from tea towels to gravestones. But this was different. This ring was like something alive, something with meaning. Kat slid the ring onto the index finger of her right hand ... the finger she had seen her great-aunt wear it on. It slipped easily over the knuckle and fitted her as if it had been made for her.

"It fits," said Kat, showing her mother.

The wind slammed at the window and the rain ran down the glass like silver claw marks. Kat's mother stood up and looked out. There was nothing to see, only a dark grey in the lowering sky, and everything a blur seen through the wind-driven rain.

"And 'Shrak' ... is that the sea dragon's name?" asked Kat, holding up the letter.

"Shrak?" said Kat's mother still staring out of the window.

"It says here 'And Shrak must sleep still and the ring be unbroken again.' Is Shrak the sea dragon from the story?" said Kat.

There was movement downstairs; the sound of men with heavy shoes moving from one room to another. Kat heard the hushed growls of Murdo and the others. She heard a woman crying and the musical *clink clink* of teacup against saucer. Suddenly the wind outside dropped and a thick drifting mist moved close to the cottage. It took shape and seemed to form itself into the sharp-toothed head of a dragon. Its grey tongue licked at the window. Kat's mother stepped back in fright. When she looked again it had gone.

"Well ...? Does the sea dragon have a name?"

"Shrak? It's a name I had forgotten until now."

"I have to go," whispered Kat.

"Go where?"

"Corrie's out there!"

Where the mist dragon's tongue had licked against the window the glass was hard-frosted over. It made no sense. Someone downstairs stumbled and fell against the banister. Kat heard the wood creak in complaint. "Steady," said Murdo sharply.

"He's out there," said Kat. She dropped her great-aunt's letter and rushed from the room.

"Wait! Katrine! Come back!"

There were men standing in the space at the

bottom of the stairs. A woman with grey in her hair was moving from one to another offering a plate of sandwiches. They broke off with their talking, looked up at Kat and stiffened. She did not stop to take in their muttered condolences, but pushed past them, darting between two tall men in dark clothes, and slipped into the living room where the women sat still nursing their china cups.

Without a word Kat exited through the back door. The bitter cold and Sal leapt on her together. Sal barked and whimpered and the cold air bit at her cheeks. Kat hurriedly untied the blue string fixed to Sal's collar and let the dog into the warm kitchen. The gate was still banging against the fence posts though there was no wind. Behind her, in a dim block of orange light, Kat saw the men relax again and heard them talking about her great-aunt and grumbling about the weather. She left the garden, pulling the black shawl up over her head and tight across her chest, and headed towards the beach.

The grey mist was everywhere, so thick you could hold it in your hand. It was like walking in a dream. There were sounds that the mist swallowed so completely that Kat doubted she was on the beach at all ... the shush of the sea breaking on the shore had never been so silent, the crunch of Kat's feet on the sand made no noise. It was so quiet that the sounds inside Kat became magnified. She heard the rasp of each laboured breath, the blood pounding in her ears. The mist spun about her taking strange shapes that dissolved again before Kat could see them, like pictures in a dream hovering just beyond recognition.

Then suddenly she was ambushed by sound returning. It roared and howled and gnashed its teeth like an angry beast. It stalked her, circling round and round her. Then the air was full of noises that stung Kat's ears, as though men were running, charging; their metal armour making a sharp and sharper dissonant music. She heard men yelling to one another, short broken warnings in a tongue she did not know. Out of the swirling mist in front of her loomed a great granite block of a man, his back to her, an enormous double-edged axe raised above his head ready to strike at anything … at nothing. Then the mist shifted and he was gone again … if he was ever really there.

Kat kept on. On either side the noise of men in armour seemed to follow her, with swords and axes ready and running in all directions. Yet something, or someone, led Kat safely through.

On and on she walked, confident of arriving at the door where she had left Corrie, walking with the certainty of one who knows absolutely that she will arrive, despite the mist that blocked her way.

The wooden door had been ripped from its two remaining hinges leaving a gaping hole in the sand. The dunes all around had altered, shifted by the earlier wind. Already the way into the tunnel was closing, small rivers of sand pouring in, cascading like water down the steps and into the blackness. Kat did not hesitate. With no wind pushing her this time, she moved forward into the dank darkness of the tunnel. The air was still and, apart from the snake-like slither of sand on the rock, it was quiet.

Kat moved to the bottom of the stone steps as if this descent into the depths was something familiar, or as if she too was being led there, just as Corrie had been led by the pull of the chess-piece magician in his hand. Though it was too dark to see, and she had no magic torch to guide her, Kat crossed straight to the low arch in the first chamber. She bent her knees, ducked her head and scuttled along the serpentine corridor that took her directly to the Hall of Forgotten Battles.

10. The Battle

A sliver of light, slight and pale, slipped between the pillars of the great hall and reached a delicate, beckoning finger through the darkness towards Kat standing at the door. On the threshold of the great chamber she paused. Somewhere was a noise … a deep-throated gargle. It was neither in front of Kat nor behind, but all around. It pressed up against her, ran its claws through her red hair and whispered in her ear.

Suddenly, the rock beneath her pitched and Kat lurched forward. She grabbed hold of the door to stop from falling on her face as Corrie had done. A surging wave swept below the tiled floor of the Hall of Forgotten Battles, heaving it into the air and driving hard against one wall, leaving the floor impossibly buckled and bowed. The pillars in the Hall of Forgotten Battles groaned like trees in a wind-tossed forest; but, with the stubbornness of trees, they held their ground.

Kat knew that Shrak had passed close by, under her very feet. There was a smell in the chamber that she knew, that she recognised. A smell she had encountered before, but today was the first time she had been able to put a name to it ... Shrak! It belonged to a memory she had only just inherited, along with the ring, but she was certain now that Shrak no longer slept. She looked at the ring on her finger. It glinted bright and yellow even in that pale light, yellow like the stirred embers of her great-aunt's fire, alive with tiny flickering flames that seemed to run around Kat's finger in an unbroken golden circle. Yet if Shrak was on the move then somehow the ring had been broken. She did not understand what that meant.

She picked her way across the uneven floor until she stood in the main body of the hall. At the far end she could see the rough cut stairway leading to the House of the Guardians. The thin light that filtered into the hall issued from within its walls. "Corrie!" Kat's voice, like her steamy breath, rose into the air and drifted away into nothing. "Are you there? Corrie?"

She moved towards the light, slowly, stopping every few steps to listen: hopeful of hearing Corrie's voice; fearful of hearing the growling that would herald Shrak's return.

As she neared the House of the Guardians, Kat saw the two carved stone warriors that flanked the door at the top of the flight of steps. A deep shadowy crack ran down the centre of one figure, splitting him in two as neatly as if he were flesh and bone, and a giant sword had crashed with titanic force down upon his brittle skull. His carved stone axe lay broken at his feet.

"Corrie!" she called, her voice flying up the steps before her.

"She has come," announced the magician, rousing Corrie from his torpor. It was as if Corrie had slept, huddled against one wall of the cold rocky chamber, as if he had slept and dreamed of chesspiece warriors passing before him, their swords and shields brandished, ready for battle.

"She has come!" the magician said again.

Corrie leapt to his feet. The shelves to either side of him were empty of chess pieces. Corrie held the magician in the air and could see that more than three walls were now empty of figures. He swept the light across the floor but the floor was empty too.

Kat stumbled on the second step. A stone piece clattered away behind her.

"Who's there?" said Corrie.

"She has come," said the magician.

Corrie took a step forward.

It was a moment of realisation. There were layers to everything in the story and words sometimes had many meanings. Corrie suddenly made sense of this one detail. "She will come" meant Shrak, that was obvious ... but it also meant Katrine. Everything was bound together, like the threads of the knot-work ring.

"Kat ..? Is that you?"

Corrie appeared at the top of the steps with the chess-piece magician held up before him.

"Kat?"

Then it was there again ... only louder. So loud

that even before it twisted under the floor of the great hall the walls cracked and the pillars quivered.

"Kat!" yelled Corrie seeing the floor of the hall undulate as a ripple beneath its surface snaked towards the House of the Guardians.

It all happened so quickly, quicker than thought. Kat was running up the steps, then falling as the floor twisted and bucked, her ringed hand reaching out to him. Corrie looked down at her. There was a moment, as though time stood frozen and everything was trapped like an insect in amber, or an image in a photograph. The black shawl had fallen back from Kat's face, her red hair fanned out like a coppery halo. Corrie could see the gold flecks in her eyes and, reflected in their grey-blue, he could see his own hand reaching out for hers. Then he saw the gold knot-work ring on her finger. He recognised it. *That was strange,* he thought, for he had not seen it before. But a part of him knew it for what it was, and like pieces in a puzzle that slowly begin to make some sort of sense, so Corrie understood that this was Katyen's ring. He grabbed instinctively at the outstretched hand and caught it. The stone steps disintegrated into rubble and dust and Kat's body smacked heavily against where the steps had been. Corrie held his grip and she did not fall.

"Are you alright?" asked Corrie when Kat clambered up into the House of the Guardians. Her legs were cut and bruised and marked with thin trails of blood.

"I'll be fine," she nodded.

"He said you would come," said Corrie.

"I had to." Kat held her hand up so that Corrie could see the Ring.

"Katyen's Ring?" said Corrie. Corrie looked closely at the ring on Kat's finger. He remembered the kneeling figure of Katyen on the tapestry and in her hand a single gold stitch — the ring. He inspected the knot-work weave of it. But the ring was not broken as he expected it to be. *The knot-work ring was broken and the magic broken too.* That's what the magician had said. Corrie was certain.

"It's Katyen's Ring," he said.

Kat nodded again. "How do you know?"

"He told me. The chess-piece magician." Corrie helped her onto her feet and they limped back to the rocky chamber. It felt somehow safer there, crouched in one corner with their arms knotted round each other.

"Do you think this is really happening?" said Kat.

Corrie shrugged. "I don't know."

The light from the chess-piece magician flickered in Corrie's hand. They both looked at the wide-eyed carved figure. Its light dulled for a second and brightened again. Corrie felt a momentary stab of cold when the light weakened, as though the magician's power had briefly left the chess piece. Then from the shadows on the other side of the cave came the sound of movement. "Shrak does not sleep," whispered Kat.

Corrie held the magician in the air. By its light they witnessed something of the magician's ancient magic. From out of the very air stepped a band of thirty or more warriors, giant men and women wearing studded leather helmets and iron breastplates. Some of them carried swords, double-bladed axes and spears with barbed heads. Others were mounted on battle horses with sharpened lances tucked under their arms. Corrie noticed that several of the warriors gnashed their broken teeth on the rims of their massive shields, and frothed and gurgled like madmen. These crazed warriors were the first through the door. With no regard to how high they were they sprang, screaming, from the House of the Guardians and disappeared into the blackness of the Hall of Forgotten Battles, rattling their weapons against their shields as they went. The mounted warriors followed in their wake, leaping into the dark, the whinnying of the frightened horses echoing in the great hall and their hooves clattering on the buckled tiled floor. The warriors that followed were more cautious, lowering each other down into the darkness. Corrie heard their armour grating against the rock and the solid thump of their feet as they landed on the torn floor of the great hall. Those below called up to the others in a strange garbled tongue, then stole away, one after the other, disappearing into the hollow blackness where the light did not reach and where the sound of splitting rock ripped the air. Then silence.

Corrie looked to the wall where the last chess pieces had stood. The shelves there were now empty, too.

They waited, straining to hear. No one spoke.

The silence stretched between them, so taught that at any moment it might break ... as easily as a dry stick. Corrie recalled Kat on the beach snapping a thin white stick in two, with a sharp and easy snap. He did not know why it was that he thought of this. The air in the chamber crackled with a fearful expectancy and the hair on Corrie's neck bristled.

His thoughts travelled back further, to the moment when he had found the chess-piece magician buried in the sand. *Was that when it had started?* he wondered, *and if so what might he be doing now if he had simply left it alone ... or if he hadn't noticed it at all?* He looked at Kat. He felt as though they had been friends for a very long time.

Her hair was tucked behind her ears, except for a single strand that had strayed and curled across one cheek. Her brow was furrowed and her lips thin. These things were familiar to him when they shouldn't have been. Like the ring on her finger, the ring with its unbroken golden braid. It was all a part of something; a part of this, a part of the whole thing. Then he knew that these thoughts were not his own. He knew that they belonged to the chess-piece even though they were in his head.

Shrak's third charge across the floor of the Hall of Forgotten Battles was the most destructive of all. Everywhere the floor churned like a black and angry sea, tossing up megalithic rocks and spitting spindrift stone tiles high into the air. Even some of the stubborn pillars were toppled. The warriors

flinched, braced themselves for battle and mur-
mured silent prayers to gods that were gone from
this world. Kat's fingers dug into Corrie's arm. He
looked again at the ring on her finger. *That was
the answer,* he thought. *That's why he had seen
it everywhere.* Something shifted and he began to
understand.

Then the warriors at the door to the House
of the Guardians were fighting. They jabbed
their swords and drilled their barbed spears into
the blackness, into something unseen but there,
swearing bitter oaths and calling down ulcerous
curses on the beast. The blackness slashed back
at them. There was nothing to see except their
swords snapping like brittle bone in their hands
and axes, swung with all the might of those giant
warriors, shattering into a thousand pieces on the
air. They fought on, even when there was nothing
left to fight with. They were not used to giving up.
They smashed their shields savagely against the
empty shadows, shivering wood and metal into
tiny splinters. They lifted great rocks above their
heads, hurling them at the darkness. Something
evil and ink-black reared up and hacked the warriors asunder with a single sudden swipe. They fell,
every one of them, like grass cut flat by the swing
of a razor-sharp scythe.

Corrie and Kat jerked back with fright and the
chess-piece magician fell from Corrie's hand. The
instant that the ivory figure touched the floor of
the House of the Guardians the room filled with
a blinding light that pierced the blackness more
sharply than a thousand spears. Somewhere in the

darkness Shrak roared in pain and shrank from
the magician's light ... and shrank from the magician too, for in the centre of the light, lit up like
an angel and suddenly as tall as the tallest giant
warrior, stood the full figure of the old magician.
He raised his staff off the ground and thumped it
down ... three times. It was like a call to order at a
grand ceremonial occasion.

In the Hall of Forgotten Battles the dragon took
shape. Where before there had been only darkness, in the brighter light now there was a hissing,
scaly creature. Her body filled the enormous hall,
her steaming coils piled one on top of the other,
rubbing against the walls and pillars. Everywhere
her slime-green scales dropped like enormous
plates, crashing on the torn rock floor. It shredded the air with its claws and growled. Corrie
saw the beast's jagged set of teeth. They were
not like the dragon's-tooth stone he had found on
the beach; each yellowed tooth was crooked and
broken ... and fiercely barbed. She tilted her head
and turned one rheumy eye on them ... inspecting
them, measuring them. The magician thumped
his staff on the ground again and a spark of light
leapt out, stabbing at the dragon's prying eye. She
recoiled screaming, her nostrils flaring, the gored
eye screwed shut.

Above the roar of the dragon came another
sound; a rhythmic pulsing sound, an ebbing and
flowing voice. At first, Corrie and Kat thought it
was singing, but could not tell where it was coming from. When the dragon paused for breath it
became obvious ... the magician was chanting. A

string of syllables, guttural and strange, spun in the air around him, rising in a widening spiral. The dragon heard it too. She cocked her head and from a distance fixed her good eye on the magician. They all watched as the magician lifted one hand into the air, as though offering something to the dragon. In the palm of his hand sat the bird ... St Francis' bird ... Noah's bird.

Recognition flickered in the dragon's blinking eye. Flexing her twisted coils, she hissed and spat. The air turned to ice. The magician flicked his hand upwards and the bird spread wide its silver wings. In its wake the magic bird trailed a fiery dust that drifted to the floor of the great hall like tiny molten sparks or embers. Where they fell on the dragon they scorched her scaly skin. The creature howled and writhed in pain, contracting her coils into a tight knot. Higher and higher the silver bird flew until it was above Shrak's monstrous head. Higher and higher until its silver feathers brushed against the vaulted rock. But it was not high enough. The dragon struck. With an angry snap of her craggy jaws she plucked the bird from the air and slowly ground its silver bones to nothing.

"You have to do something," said Corrie.

Kat stiffened. "Me?" she said incredulously.

"You have to. He can't do it on his own ... He said so."

The dragon snorted a scornful icy blast down on the magician.

"What can *I* do?" Kat was shivering.

"You have the ring," said Corrie.

"Katyen's Ring," said Kat holding it up.

"She helped last time. The magician told me."

"But what can a ring do?" said Kat.

"I don't know. The ring must be magic .... it must be more powerful than the magician."

The magician gripped the end of his staff in both hands. He raised it above his head and then brought it crashing down on the ground. A zig-zag rope of flame whipped into the darkness, lashing at the dragon's neck. Shrak snorted and bellowed and stamped her titan paws over the blaze until its fire was snuffed out.

"But how does it work?"

The dragon bent her head level with the doorway and breathed its cold breath into the chamber. The empty shelves of rock where the chess-piece guardians had stood cracked and fell. Corrie saw the magician's shoulders slacken, his back bow and his head fall forward.

"We have to help!" Stirred by an ancient memory, something that had passed from the magician's thoughts into his, Corrie knew he had to act. It was something the magician had said; something about Corvald the Rower bringing the pieces together. That was his role. It seemed to make sense now. The ring was many things. It was Katyen's ring with its magic. It was Shrak bound into a knot. And it was something else ... something to do with the three of them: with the magician, Corvald and Katyen standing together; three strands woven into one. Now Corrie and Kat were to stand with the magician, weaving again what had been broken. That was the ring that needed to be re-formed. It made sense.

Corrie took Kat's hand and dragged her into the centre of the magician's bright circle. The light brightened, like a prolonged flash of lightning. Shrak screamed and cowered away from the House of the Guardians. Without knowing why he did it, Corrie reached for the magician's hand. The moment he did so a strange thing happened. It was as though an electrical charge leapt between Kat and the magician and Corrie, and back again. The three became one. Their thoughts became a shared knowledge passing from one to the other, weaving in and out, like the three strands of the knot-work ring.

"The ring is mended!"

The magician drew himself back to his full height and he turned towards the dragon. They all faced the dragon, the one uninterrupted thought threading through them … the ring that was broken is whole once more … the dragon must sleep again.

The magician struck his staff on the rock floor one last time. This time a thick girdle of flame, blue, red and yellow, wrapped itself around Shrak … not once or twice, but three times. It twisted and turned to form a braided ring of flame that was without beginning or end. The dragon wailed, shaking the roof of the Hall of Forgotten Battles and renting it in two. The grey sky was suddenly visible through a ragged gash in the rock. The dragon tightened her coils, shrinking from the ring of flame, twisting and turning in on herself, writhing until her scaly body was tied in tortuous knots. The monster's tail had fallen outside the flaming circle and flicked against one of the remaining rock pillars. The pillar crashed and tumbled to the floor.

"The ring," yelled Corrie. Before the words were out, the thought had passed between them so that it was as if they had yelled as one. Corrie recalled the braid ring on the box he had found on the beach. He saw the shadow of the ring embossed on the fly-leaf of the Gaelic book that contained the sea dragon's tale. Then, Katyen's ring, running in a plaited golden band round Kat's index finger. Now, the interwoven ring of thought bound Corrie, Kat and the magician together, while the ring of fire encircled Shrak's coils. So many rings.

Shrak's loose tail swung savagely against the entrance to the House of the Guardians, like a dropped stitch that threatened to unravel the whole pattern. It slashed wildly at another pillar and part of the ceiling fell. The floor shook beneath their feet and a noise like thunder rolled around the rocky chamber. Corrie looked down at the cracks appearing on the cave floor. And that's when he saw it … the embroidered ring round the hem of the magician's robe. Braided the same as all the other rings, but different too … different in the way that the ring of iron on the door to the Hall of Forgotten Battles was different. It was Shrak's Ring and it was unbroken. A dragon's tail caught in a dragon's mouth.

They each knew what had to be done.

"The tail! Get the tail!" the children yelled together.

Shrak thrashed her loose tail down on the floor of the Hall of Forgotten Battles sending a ripple through the rock. The cracks beneath their feet deepened, splitting the floor in three places. Already they were moving, down into the great hall.

Shrak hissed and spat and screamed at them from inside the ring of flame. She drew back her tail and might have broken the circle forever, but the magician began beating the scaly tail with his staff, as once before, in another story, he had beaten Shrak's head. The dragon roared and snarled at them and her tail, as thick as two men, fell limp at their feet. Still the magician thrashed his staff down upon the dragon's scales and the dragon's roaring cut the air, tearing down the last pillars in the hall, clawing at the walls.

When Shrak could stand it no more, she jerked her head through the ring of flame, snapping her teeth at the magician's staff. In the same instant, Kat and Corrie dropped hands, leaped forward and lifted the dragon's limp tail into the air. Shrak's teeth clamped tightly over her own tail and the last circle was complete. A grim choking sounded from the dragon and then, as though no more substantial than a fading dream, Shrak dissolved into empty air.

Above them the ceiling groaned and began to crumble and on every side the walls of the Hall of Forgotten Battles splintered and cracked. Kat and Corrie turned to where the magician had stood but the light had died and he was gone ... part of the same insubstantial dream as the dragon.

"C'mon!" Kat grabbed Corrie's hand and, running

and stumbling, they clambered over the broken tiled floor, out through the door and along the low-ceilinged passage. Behind them rock clapped against rock, exploding with deep thundering moans. Stone folded over stone, stone on stone. As they reached the final steps that led back to the beach a terrible tremble ran through the ground and the flight of stairs crackled like a winter bonfire.

"Run!" yelled Kat.

The rock fractured underneath them and the steps fell away behind them. Up and up they ran, urgently … not daring to look back, their legs heavy and tired. Being one step ahead had never meant so much. Onwards and upwards they fled towards the small square of light that was there somewhere at the top staircase. Each footstep a slow agony as their muscles tightened and their bodies strained.

"Keep going," screamed Corrie, or maybe it was Kat who called out, or maybe it was the voice of the magician rising to meet them from the dark depths behind them.

Just ahead of him Kat tripped and Corrie stumbled after her. They struggled to get up but their bodies suddenly found air. Then they were falling backwards into the dark dust.

Far below them the Hall of Forgotten Battles collapsed in on itself with a final echoing sigh. A fat-cheeked bubble of air escaped from the flattened chamber. It pumped through the low passage and, catching Kat and Corrie in its soft airy kiss, lifted them up the last few steps and spat them out onto the white sand of Uig.

11. After the Storm

The grey clouds cleared on a blue sky and the mist swept up off the beach away beyond the purple hills. Kat and Corrie lay still, side by side, not yet able to move, barely able to breathe. The sand on their cheeks felt soft as a pillow and the sea, lapping gently against the shore, muttered a hushed wordless whisper. Somewhere a lapwing screamed an excited *pee-whit* and received a shrill *pee-whit* back for an answer. Corrie saw the two birds cartwheeling clumsily across the sky, clumsily but the one perfectly mirroring the other, just as Kat and Corrie had flown through the air to land on the beach. He smiled. A big-faced sun reached down and stroked warm soft fingers over his back.

"Kat?" said Corrie, without opening his eyes.

There was no reply.

Kat sat up. Looking back along the beach it was as if nothing had happened at all. She saw the same skewed line of cottages stretching away to her great-aunt's, the same square windows staring unblinking out to sea, and the same squat chimneys breathing out slow lazy spirals of thin smoke.

"Are you alright?" Corrie asked, still not moving.

It *was* like waking from a dream. Kat hugged her knees into the ring of her arms. The bruises were real enough, she thought. A dusting of sand stuck to the blood from her cuts. She brushed away the clotted grains. "I'm fine. You okay?"

Corrie opened his eyes

"It's over, isn't it?"

Kat nodded. "I think so."

He lay still, counting each breath, not sure what had really happened in the end, not sure how they had escaped from the collapsing staircase. The battle with Shrak seemed even more like a dream to him.

"Did it really happen?" he said.

Kat did not reply. She was staring past Corrie to a deep black cut in the curl of Uig bay.

Corrie lifted his head and saw it too ... a giant hole sunk in the beach. Already it was filling with sand and with each swell the sea spilled over the broken stone, hissing and gurgling.

The Hall of Forgotten Battles, thought Corrie. He thought of all the tapestries that had been lost and their stories, too. He thought of the empty space that had been left for the tapestry that would record the last battle with Shrak, the battle they had just won ... only now there would be no more tapestries. Tomorrow the hole that marked where the hall had been would be no more than a shallow basin, and the day after that it would be a scarcely visible scar on the arc of Uig Bay.

They walked in silence most of the way back. Corrie stopped only to drag storm-dropped driftwood clear of the high water mark, in case he had to collect firewood later. Kat watched him wrestle with splintered planks and heavy torn beams.

"Isn't this how it all started?" she said smiling.

Corrie looked up, returning her smile with a shrug of his shoulders and let fall the piece of wood from his grasp.

They halted at the wall bordering the bottom of Corrie's drive. It was awkward between them. They both looked away, each searching a different sweep of the landscape for something to say.

Coming out of the cottage at the far end of the village Corrie could see a procession of men dressed in dark suits and carrying high on their shoulders Kat's great-aunt's coffin. Behind them trailed the other mourners in a ragged train.

"You'd better go," he said.

Kat turned to where he looked. Her mother was directly behind the coffin. Kat straightened the hem of her dress and brushed her fingers through the tangles of her hair. It was only then that she noticed that she had lost her great aunt's black shawl.

"I expect I should join them. I thought it'd be over by now."

She hung back, watching the procession as it turned slowly towards a low-walled plot of ground that served as a graveyard.

"She'd like it that the sun was out ... my great-aunt. That's what she wanted at the end."

Corrie nodded, not sure what to say.

Together they watched the knot of mourners as it moved away from them.

"I don't really believe in dragons," said Corrie, at last.

Without looking at him, Kat shook her head. "That makes sense. Not many people do."

"As for sea dragons …" scoffed Corrie, kicking over several of the moss cloaked gravel chips that lined the drive.

"They just exist in stories," said Kat.

"Like magic chess pieces."

"Yeah."

Corrie stared down at the scuffed toe of his boot. "Best keep it to ourselves then, don't you think?" he said.

Kat nodded.

"Nobody would believe us anyway," said Corrie.

"Except maybe my mum." Kat looked at him. "Some of it she might."

"Mum … short for mumbo-jumbo," laughed Corrie.

"Maybe," said Kat, and she laughed too.

Corrie watched her as she played with her aunt's gold ring … Katyen's ring, her ring now. He wanted to say something, but the words stuck in his mouth.

Kat reached into the pocket of her dress. She took Corrie's hand in hers and folded something into his palm, closing his fingers over it as though it was a secret she was sharing with him.

"Well …," she said beginning to back away from him.

"Well ...," replied Corrie, not sure whether he should look at what she had gifted him.

"I'll go."

Corrie nodded, still lost for words.

Their thoughts reached out towards each other but, without the chess-piece magician, they didn't quite connect.

"See you," said Kat, then turned and walked off.

"Yeah ... you will," he answered.

This time Kat shrugged.

"See you tomorrow?" Corrie called.

He turned to go and then remembered something. "You still haven't told me about the Viking treasure," he called after her.

She did not reply. He wondered if she'd heard him. He watched her run back along the hamlet's crooked street, the red flag of her hair flapping behind her.

Then he opened the closed fist of his hand. There, to his surprise, was a single chess-piece figure ... not the magician, but a Beserker, his bared teeth resting on the rim of his shield and his wild eyes staring. *She must have collected it from the floor of the Hall of Guardians,* he thought. He slipped the carved ivory chessman into his pocket.

In the cottage Corrie leaned against one wall, put the toe of one boot to the heel of the other and eased it loose in a practised move. He flicked his foot and sent the boot neatly into the corner, then did the same to the other boot, before netting one of the curled coat hooks with the hood of his jacket on his second attempt.

"Is that you, Corr?"

"Yes, Mum," said Corrie padding across the flagstone floor and into the large kitchen. Corrie's father was at the table reading yesterday's newspaper, half listening to the static hiss and crackle of the old radio. His mother was kneeling in front of the fireplace. She had fashioned a wigwam out of stunted sticks and balled paper and was about to strike a long match over the roughened side of a yellow and red matchbox.

"Soaked to the skin, I shouldn't wonder," she said, looking up at Corrie. His brown hair was flattened to his head, almost dry now. He looked pale.

"Did you get caught out in that storm?" asked his father.

"I had my jacket," said Corrie, side-stepping the question.

"That was some piece of freak weather. There's been nothing about it on the radio. Jane was certain that it was going to be fine today and the sun's shining now. Freezing mist and rain and angry winds one minute and the next it was all gone. Very strange."

"Where have you been?" said Corrie's mother. "We were worried about you."

"It's warm out now," said Corrie. *Jane could be both right and wrong at the same time,* he thought. He edged behind the sofa and over to the chair, slumping heavily into its cushioned arms. He winced, the bruises causing a dull ache in his legs and his back.

"You look a bit stiff in the legs there, Corrie," teased his father.

"All that cycling," said Corrie's mother sitting back on her heels to watch her wigwam bursting into blue flame. She brushed her hair from her brow with the back of one wrist. "We're not used to it. I'm a bit stiff myself. Tired too."

He let them think what they wanted. He knew that they would not accept the truth, even if he were able to tell them. The truth could not be fitted into one of his father's holiday photographs. He closed his eyes, feeling the soft tug of sleep. He thought about the chess-piece magician and the chess-piece warriors leaping into the blackness to do battle; he thought of the plaited rings of the sea dragon and the buried Hall of Forgotten Battles with its lost commemorative tapestries. Sitting there in the cottage kitchen, with the small fire slowly crackling into life and the crinkle of his father's newspaper, Corrie wasn't sure *he* believed it either. *Sometimes the truth belonged more to the realm of dream,* he thought.

"We'll have an easier day tomorrow, if you like. See what Jane says about the weather. If it's like this we could picnic on the beach." Corrie's father returned to his newspaper.

"We could ask that girl up the road." His mother bowed before the burning paper and sticks and fanned the flames with a blown prayer. "I expect she'll need cheering up after her aunt's funeral. Her name's Katrine."

"'Kat' for short," said Corrie opening his eyes for a moment.

His parents exchanged looks of surprise.

"I'll ask her, if you like," said Corrie, yawning and closing his eyes again, before giving in to sleep and the dreams that sleep would bring.

Lari Don

First Aid for Fairies and Other Fabled Beasts

'*Lari Don is the next big thing in the world of
children's books.*'
— STV

Helen has absolutely no interest in becoming a vet like
her mother. So she isn't best pleased when asked to
help an injured horse. Only this horse isn't entirely
normal ... and nor are his friends.

Without warning, Helen is thrust into an extraordi-
nary world full of magical rituals, fantastical creatures
and a dangerous, powerful beast known as the Master,
who would destroy it all.

Winner of the Kelpies Prize
Nominated for the Royal Mail Award for Scottish Children's Books

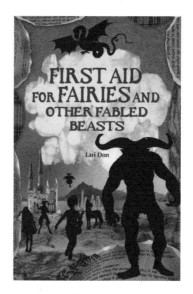

Kelpies

Lari Don

Wolf Notes and Other Musical Mishaps

Helen has won a place at a prestigious summer music school in remote north-western Scotland. But as she practises for a concert on Midsummer's Eve, her friends, the fabled beasts, prepare for battle — in the very forest where the young musicians are staying.

When Yann the centaur arrives and warns Helen of impending danger, Helen finds herself catapulted into a perilous quest, allied with fantastical creatures against a powerful enemy, the Faerie Queen.

This is the magical sequel to the bestselling *First Aid for Fairies and Other Fabled Beasts*.

Kelpies

Mike Nicholson

Catscape

'*A well-paced, entirely convincing mystery novel, full
of suspense, wit and unexpected twists and turns.*'
— School Librarian

Fergus can't believe it when his brand-new digital
watch starts going backwards. Then he crashes
(literally) into gadget-loving Murdo and a second mystery comes to light: cats are going missing all over the
neighbourhood.

Sharply and wittily observed, this is a story of unlikely
friendships, unexpected allies and cat surveillance.

Winner of the Kelpies Prize

Kelpies

Mike Nicholson

Grimm

If you have the misfortune to spend a night at Hotel Grimm, it may be the last one you spend anywhere! From its vantage point high above the town, the hotel has long been the source of terrifying stories.

When eleven-year-old Rory McKenna becomes an overnight advertising sensation for Zizz Cola, Hotel Grimm's mysterious owner, Granville Grimm, presents Rory with the task of giving his hotel a new image. Refusal is not an option ...

Will he become Hotel Grimm's next victim? Rory's life is about to get very complicated.

Kelpies

Annemarie Allan

Hox

*'This is a superb, intelligent and gripping novel. The
strange bond between a boy and an animal draws you in
and you will be desperate to know what happens next.'*
— Waterstone's Guide to Children's Books

Faced with a cold Saturday afternoon stuck at the
Institute for Animal Research, Robbie is angry and
frustrated. Then a disturbing encounter in the animal
house thrusts him into a perilous journey through the
stunning but inhospitable landscape of a Highland
winter.

Winner of the Kelpies Prize
Nominated for the Royal Mail Award for Scottish Children's Books

Kelpies

Annemarie Allan

Breaker

Tom and Beth are not happy when they move to North Berwick and find themselves facing a rainy, windswept beach, a house that's falling to pieces and a school full of strangers. When they meet Professor Macblain, with his weird and wonderful inventions, little do they know that he has a secret: not only is he a thief, but he has stolen the one thing that can save the Firth of Forth from environmental catastrophe.

A daring adventure unfolds in this funny and fast-paced tale of disasters waiting to happen.

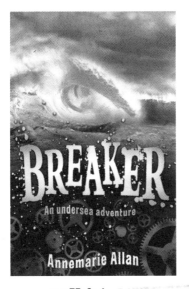

Kelpies

Sharon Tregenza

Tarantula Tide

*'This is Enid Blyton with iPods
and lashings of coke'*
— The Shetland Times

Smugglers. Vikings. Shetland should be a fascinating place for a holiday, but Jack is harbouring a secret and is less than enthusiastic to be there. Then he meets Izzie and her exotic pets and things soon start to get more interesting.

Jack and Izzie unwittingly find themselves in the middle of a dangerous adventure, wondering what the next tide will bring to the land of the Viking Fire Festival.

Winner of the Kelpies Prize

Kelpies

ST PETER THE APOSTLE
HIGH SCHOOL